Fury Trail

Center Point Large Print

This Large Print Book carries the
Seal of Approval of N.A.V.H.

Fury Trail

GILES A. LUTZ

CENTER POINT PUBLISHING
THORNDIKE, MAINE

This Center Point Large Print edition
is published in the year 2008 by arrangement with
Golden West Literary Agency.

The text of this Large Print edition is unabridged. In other
aspects, this book may vary from the original edition.
Printed in the United States of America.
Set in 16-point Times New Roman type.

ISBN: 978-1-60285-217-4

Library of Congress Cataloging-in-Publication Data

Lutz, Giles A.
    Fury trail / Giles A. Lutz.--Center Point large print ed.
        p. cm.
    ISBN-13: 978-1-60285-217-4 (lib. bdg. : alk. paper)
    1. Large type books. I. Title.

PS3562.U83F87 2008
813'.54--dc22

2008004911

Chapter One

THE short, chunky man nervously chewed his lower lip. He was attracting attention here, and that was the last thing he wanted. He looked up, and the bartender was staring at him. He returned the stare until the bartender looked away. Those two at the end of the bar were talking about him, too. He caught their covert glances at him before they put their heads together. The questions he had been asking around here were bound to attract notice, he knew. After tonight, though, it would make no difference. He filled a glass with whisky and recklessly drank it to drown his mounting apprehension. He was close to something; he felt a tingling warning in the atmosphere.

He drummed impatiently on the table with broad fingers. He was waiting for the dancehall girl called Susie to come on duty. He grimaced faintly at the thought of her. She was hard-faced and weary looking, and any good points she might have had had faded under the wear and tear of her life. She had reached the age where she was desperate for attention, and he had preyed upon her loneliness to gain the information he needed. He was not proud of the fact, but she worked here, and a woman could pry where a man dared not. If he could put a different name to the bearded man who owned this place, a long, hard hunt would be over.

The whisky had no power to lift him. He was tired,

to the very marrow of his bones. He wondered if he had been wrong in writing Ross that he felt he was on the right track. Ross had been so positive he would find his man somewhere in the vicinity of San Francisco. That letter would pull him to Virginia City as fast as he could come. Perhaps he should have waited until he had something more definite than suspicion. He closed his fist and looked at it, knowing an almost insane desire to smash it into the wall. He forced his fist open and tried to relax. The two men at the bar gave him a final look before they moved to the door.

The waiting was agony, but he had to know if the bearded man who called himself Zachary Tanner was actually Gary Anson.

What would he do if Susie's information were positive? He wanted to go ahead and finish this, but he knew he would not until Ross got here. Ross had earned the right to face Anson again. The quicker that moment came, the quicker he could return to the life he and Ross Stone had known before this began. How many useless hours had he spent in arguing with his younger brother to forget this hunt? But when a man was filled with hatred, there was room for nothing else. He remembered the day Ross had told him he was going after Anson, and it was as vivid as though it were happening now. He had looked at the hard set of Ross's face and the tortured misery in his eyes and said quietly, "All right, Ross. Two of us can cover more country." He had thought that a few weeks, months at the most, would turn up Anson. But Anson had been a frightened man, and his fear had lent speed and trickery to his feet.

Two years, he thought gloomily. Two years torn out of their lives for no purpose. He had seen Ross five times during that period, and each time with nothing to report but false leads. But this time his questions had turned up a hornet's nest. For a day and a half he had been under surveillance, and why that, unless someone was afraid?

He emptied the last of the bottle into his glass and slowly drank it. Memory was a slippery thing, and after two years he was not positive he could identify Anson. This one, who called himself Tanner, might or might not be Anson. The beard and the name were wrong, but beards could be grown, and a name changed as easily as a man slipped into a different shirt.

The saloon was crowded, and he heard raucous laughter from the men thronged at the bar. Somewhere in the back of the room a woman laughed in a high, brittle voice. He wondered what was keeping Susie. She should have been here a half hour ago.

He was getting to his feet when he saw her pushing through the crowd. He settled back in his chair, watching her. A man reached out and pawed her bare shoulder, and she slapped the hand away. Another dangled a bulging buckskin pouch before her, and she did not see it.

He felt a mounting excitement. Something had happened to make her blind to invitations that were her bread and butter.

She stopped at his table, and he saw the bright glitter in her eyes. Her breast rose and fell in the intensity of some inner emotion. Even at her best, she had never been a beautiful woman, and this life had squeezed her like a sponge, leaving her dry and brittle. Her face was too thin, too angular, and paint failed to cover the ravages of time and events. Her dress was cut low in an attempt to draw men's eyes to charms that were fast fading. Her eyes were tired, desperately so.

He felt a pity for her and a shame for himself. But he needed the information her manner told him she had. He put warmth into his voice and said, "I've been waiting a long time."

She leaned over the table to grasp his hand, and the low bodice revealed the valley between her breasts. She said in a panting voice, "Come outside. I can't talk to you here."

"You found out?"

Her nod was an abrupt, jerky motion, and an inward sigh flooded him. He had not been wrong in sending Ross that letter.

He stood up, noticing the barkeep watching him. He reached out and tucked her hand under his arm. He moved with her to the door and thought it would look all right to appear in a hurry. There were many woman-starved men in Virginia City.

They stepped outside, and he said eagerly, "What is it, Susie?"

She shook her head and tightened her hand on his arm, leading him down the block. Even at this hour the street was teeming with traffic. Heavy ore wagons lumbered along, raising a choking blanket of dust that settled slowly in their wake. Riders galloped up and down the street, and the walks were crowded with men pushing from one saloon to another, seeking excitement and diversion. Somewhere up ahead a shot sounded, but very few heads turned in that direction. Virginia City was wild and rough, and the sound of a shot was hardly enough to interrupt a man's thoughts.

He moved along with her, wondering where she was taking him. Not to her living quarters, he hoped. If she wanted kindness and affection in return for her information, it would be a stiff price. Perhaps the little money he had in his pocket would satisfy her.

She turned at the head of the block, and it was darker on the side street. He said, "Susie," and she whispered, "Wait!"

"In here," she said as they approached the dark mouth of an alley.

He stepped ahead of her, and after the wash of light on the street, the alley was very dark. Two shadows broke off from the main body of the blackness and were upon him before he was even sure there was movement.

The hard ring of a gun barrel prodded into the small of his back, and a harsh voice said, "Just hold it."

The other gun did not touch him, but he could sense its presence. A hand closed about the butt of his gun and jerked it from its holster. He heard the plop as it was thrown down the alley. He felt naked and afraid.

He turned his head. to look at the woman. Her face was a blurred, pale oval in the darkness. He said, "You bitch."

She spat full into his face, and her laugh sounded like the crumpling of stiff paper. "You fool," she said mockingly. "Did you think I was falling for you?"

"Shut up, Susie," the harsh voice commanded.

The gun barrel dug deeper into his back, and he moved ahead in response to its order. "In here," the voice growled after they had gone a hundred yards.

His throat was tight, and his heart was painfully thumping. He judged they were in back of the saloon he had just left. He had been so sure of Susie that he had ignored the little warning signs that pointed toward danger. He stumbled as his boot caught on the first step. The heel of a hand slammed into his shoulder, knocking him to his knees, and the edge of a step cut into them.

"Get up, you bastard," the voice said.

A door opened before him, whining on its hinges, and he was shoved into a short corridor that led to a narrow flight of stairs. He walked up the stairs, and a door at the head of them was open. He stepped into an office furnished with a battered roll-top desk and an equally battered swivel chair. Two straight-backed chairs made up the rest of the furnishings. The plank flooring had warped, gaping widely in places. His eyes followed one of the cracks, trying to fill his mind with its course. It was a poor, feeble effort to keep from thinking of other things.

The silence held for a long moment. He felt the impact of five pairs of eyes. He turned his head once for a quick glance at the two men who had picked him up in the alley. They were the same two that had stood at the end of the bar. He knew Susie and Tanner, the tall, bearded man. The other he had never seen before.

Tanner took a cheroot from his mouth, moistened its length and studied it before he spoke. "Tate," he said to the stranger standing beside him. "This is the one who has been asking all the questions."

Tate's face was devoid of expression. It was as white and hard as though it had been carved out of marble. He had cold, cruel eyes with an unblinking stare. He said, "Maybe he never learned it ain't nice to ask questions."

Tanner looked full at the prisoner with blazing eyes. His nose was long and slightly hooked. He had full mobile lips. The beard hid his chin and jaws. "Who are you?" he demanded. His voice was sharp, almost brittle.

The prisoner wet his lips before he answered. "I'm Tom Jones," he said huskily. "What's this all about? If a man can't come into your place looking for a little fun—" He looked at the woman, then back at Tanner. "Hell," he protested. "I didn't know I was doing any trespassing."

The fire in Tanner's eyes increased. "You lying son of a bitch," he rasped. He nodded, and a gun rose swiftly in one of the hands of the two men behind the prisoner. The prisoner turned his head, and his eyes

11

went wide at sight of the down-sweeping arm. The light exploded into a million shooting stars, then faded quickly into blackness, and he did not know he pitched forward on his face.

He came to, seated in one of the straight-backed chairs. His chin hung on his chest, and there was pain now, pain that threatened to tear off the top of his head. It was a moment before he realized his hands were tied behind him. The fear swelled large enough inside him to make him forget the pain.

Tanner seized his hair and jerked up his head. He said, "You could save yourself a lot of trouble."

The man in the chair forced his eyes to lock with Tanner's. Fear was freezing his thoughts. He formed his words with deliberate care. "I don't know what you're talking about," he said.

Tanner pulled on his cheroot until the end was glowing, and then pressed it against the bound man's cheekbone. The other hand held his hair so that he could not move his head.

The pain was sickening. He wanted to yell from the agony of it, and he bit hard against his lower lip to stop from crying out.

Tanner ground the cigar into the flesh until it shattered in his hand. He flung it away and said, "What's your real name?"

The bound man closed his eyes. The smell of his burned flesh made him nauseous.

Tanner's voice sounded as though it came from far

away. "He still thinks he's tough," he said. "You'd better whittle some of that toughness away, Tate."

The prisoner opened his eyes. Susie's face was strained and white, and the back of a hand was pressed hard against her lips. The others watched with cruel curiosity.

Tate said, "I'm the best whittling man there is." His eyes were hard and shining with eagerness. His hand moved, and the knife appeared in it as though by magic. He glided toward the chair with the stealth of a snake.

The prisoner's throat was locked with tightness. At the moment, no possible sound could have passed through it. His eyes were fixed in horrible fascination on the advancing knife-point.

He threw back his head at its touch, and his body arched as far as the rope would permit it. The fiery line started in his upper arm and traced a course almost to his elbow. He could not stop his groan.

Tanner bent forward, watching him. "What's your name? What are you after here?"

The prisoner looked dully at his sleeve, already soaked with blood.

Susie made an odd whimpering sound. "No, Zachary," she moaned.

Tanner whirled on her, an excess of rage twisting his face. "God damn you," he shouted. "Shut up."

She gave no indication that she heard him. Her moans kept up.

Tanner seized her arm and slapped her, first on one

side of the face, then on the other. Each slap was a hard, savage blow, each one drove the blood from her face and rocked her head.

Her cries died into the whimpering. "Don't," she gasped. Tanner spun her toward the door. "Get out of here," he yelled. He shoved her, and the force of it knocked her down.

She looked up at him, her eyes big. "I'm sorry," she whispered. "It was seeing the blood. I didn't mean to—"

"Get out," he shouted.

She whirled and stumbled blindly out of the door.

Tanner turned back toward the man in the chair. The grip of his rage made him look insane. "Who are you here for? Is it Ross Stone? Is he here?" His voice went up several notches. "Answer me, damn you, or I'll let Tate cut you to pieces."

The prisoner stared at him with clearing eyes. All his questions were answered. This was Gary Anson, standing before him. He should have put a name in that letter he wrote to Ross, but the letter would bring Ross here, and that should be all that was necessary.

"It took us a long time to find you, didn't it?" he asked in a low voice. His fear was gone now. He was facing the inevitable and it left no room for fear. He knew what was going to happen to him. It was in the bearded man's eyes, in the eagerness on Tate's face. He knew some regrets. He had so wanted to return to the life he and Ross had known.

He said, taunting, "Ross is coming, Anson. You gonna run some more, or wait? If you wait, you know what will happen, don't you?"

Tanner looked as though he were choking. "Damn it," he managed in a ragged voice. "I should have seen it. You're Cleve Stone."

The man in the chair nodded mockingly. "Run again, Anson. Run while you got the chance."

Tanner's face went maniacal. He seized the knife from Tate's hand. The light glittered on the blade at the top of its arc. The downward stroke was a flashing streak of light. The blade drove in deep under the breast bone. A shattered cry escaped the bound man's lips. His body arched against its bonds, then slumped back into the chair, dead.

Tate said in a complaining voice, "Hell, that was quick." He flexed the fingers of his right hand.

Tanner looked at the other two men in the room and said, "Get out."

They looked at him, at the dead man, then back to him. They turned without a word and moved toward the door.

Tanner waited until it closed behind them. "Tate, I want you to ride to Folsom. Ross Stone will come through there. He's a big bastard, and he's got the coldest blue eyes a man ever saw. He's black-headed and has a three-cornered scar on the right side of his chin. I want you to kill him."

Tate looked at him with curiosity filled eyes. "You're pretty scared of him, ain't you, Zach?" He glanced at the limp form in the chair. "What was that name he called you?"

Tanner's face turned raging again. "I'll give you some advice, Tate. As long as you're working for me, you keep your damned nose out of my personal business. You hear me?"

Tate laughed softly. "Sure, Zach. I won't let this Stone get near you."

Tanner's hands closed into tight fists. "You ought to get there before him. Meet every train that comes in. Don't come back until you get him. Send those two back in here. I want them to carry this thing out."

Tate strolled to the door. He paused with his hand on the knob. "I'll give you some advice, Zach. Don't push a woman around too much. They can hurt you worse than any man."

Chapter Two

ROSS STONE waited patiently for an opening in the milling crowd on the station platform at Folsom. It was an irritable crowd; the train ride from Sacramento to here had strained tempers thin. The road was rough and the seats hard. Passengers had the option of keeping coach windows closed and suffocating with the heat, or leaving them open and choking to death on the dirty, foul-smelling smoke from the engine.

He leaned against the station wall, big and easy-appearing to the casual eye. It would have taken a keen observer to notice that the whiplash energy of the man was barely controlled.

He did not like cities or crowds, and in the past months he had been thrown in contact with both too many times. For two years, he had been scrutinizing every face he saw in the weakening hope that he would see the one he sought. How many times had he worried about the course he was following—and admitted that it might be useless? Yet he could not let go of it. The hatred within him was too strong. It kept him fixed, like an animal on a scent.

He watched the milling, unhappy crowd. The fact that the train was four hours late and had missed the connection by stage to Virginia City was the final straw. Men cursed the railroad, the engineer and train crew, and most of all, the stages for not waiting. Sheep, he thought bitterly. The well-dressed city men were the worst. They expected the same kind of service here that they were used to in the cities. The poorly dressed men were timid and uncertain, bunching together for mutual support. The women in crinoline, silks, and satins were equally out of place. They dabbed at their faces with dainty handkerchiefs and fretted over the handling of their baggage.

It was not difficult to spot the men who belonged in the wilderness. They were dressed in rough clothing, and the heat and dust had not twisted their faces into angry masks. Half a dozen women, standing in a little group to one side, would also fit the life ahead of them. They showed a bold expanse of ankle, and their gaudy silk dresses displayed too much shoulder and too much throat. The brawling, lusty Washoe would appreciate that kind of women much more than their proper, sedate sisters. Heads turned and calculating glances washed over the women, and each glance was met with bold invitations from unabashed eyes.

He had not changed his position for quite a while, and no strain or impatience showed in his face. His skin was beaten and sun-browned, the jaw was a sharp, harsh line. His mouth seemed cut wide for laughter but there was no humor in it now. His nose was hawklike, flaring slightly at the nostrils, and his blue eyes were deep and well-spaced above it. A broad-brimmed hat was pushed carelessly back, showing black hair faintly filmed with dust. A scar stood out prominently on the right side of his jaw, the result of a gouging branch as he had ridden through brush. He was dressed in riders' clothes, the boots well worn, the heels slightly run over. When he straightened, he would tower over every man on the platform. He was broad in the shoulders and lean in the flanks, and there was an air of hard, sure competence about him. His face was impassive, his reserve complete.

He felt eyes upon him and turned his head. There were dozens of pairs of eyes upon the platform, and many had momentarily touched him. But this touch was different. This scrutiny had an interest in it that was as tangible as a nudge.

He saw a short, compact man with a cold, white

face. The whiteness of the skin was misleading, placing him as belonging to a city. His clothes were fancifully cut, and that was misleading, too. But he fitted here, and he would fit in an even more rough locale. There was a sureness about the man, even an aura of danger. Ross did not miss the calculating squint of the eyes, nor the tied-down holster. This man was interested in him beyond a casual degree.

He held his gaze until the man shifted his eyes. A warning tingle ran through his veins. The crowd closed, blocking his view. He stared thoughtfully in the direction of the man for a long time. He was quite sure he would see him again.

The crowd drifted toward the business district, seeking accommodations, and Ross waited until the last of them had gone. He wanted to talk to one of the stageline officials and ask the questions that had become so old through repetition. He moved to the section of the platform where the stages loaded. It was empty, and the stage office was closed. Ross had been afraid of that when he learned how late the train was.

A man passed, pushing a loaded baggage truck ahead of him, and Ross stopped him. He said, "Pardon me," in a slow drawl.

The frown of irritation that was forming faded as the man appraised Ross's size. He said, "Can I help you?"

Ross asked, "Have you seen a woman pass through Folsom?" He wished he knew Anson's description, but he had seen him only once and could remember no outstanding trait about him. Besides, in a country where men predominated, a woman would be more easily remembered.

"This woman is small," he went on. He touched his upper biceps. "Standing about here. She has blue eyes and the blondest hair a man ever saw." That gave him a twist, recalling that. He remembered the feel of it during the first, few happy months.

The baggage handler shook his head. "Lots of women pass through here, mister."

"She had a mole on her left cheek. Something like a beauty mark."

"She come in recently?"

Ross shook his head. "I don't know. It could have been six months ago."

The man's snort was almost derisive. "Hell, if I saw her, I wouldn't remember that far back. Ask the baggage master tomorrow. He sees more people than I do, and he's got an eye out for any woman." He started the truck, his interest in the subject gone.

Ross knew no particular disappointment at the negative answer. He had grown used to them. Perhaps his asking the man was more habit than anything else. But he had heard that Folsom was the funnel for Virginia City and that eighty per cent of the people headed there would leave from Folsom. He had Cleve's letter, saying it looked as though the trail ended in Virginia City.

He looked at the sinking sun and decided against buying a horse and riding on to Virginia City that night. It would be dark in a couple of hours at the most, and a strange mountain trail was no place to be at night.

He picked up his bedroll and moved toward the business district. The first two hotels were filled by the time he reached them.

The clerk at the second one grinned and said, "The town always does a good business when the train's late, mister. You might try Mrs. Wesley's. She has a room she lets out sometimes. She's around the corner from here."

Ross nodded his thanks and walked out of the lobby. He turned the corner, and Mrs. Wesley's house was a small, dingy white frame building. He turned before he knocked on the door, and his instinct was right. The man who had stared at him so long on the station platform was going down the other side of the street. He was not looking at Ross, but Ross felt it was no mere accident that brought the man this way. He watched until the man turned the corner, and the crawly feeling along his skin was more pronounced.

He said to himself, "That'll bear watching," and knocked on the door.

Mrs. Wesley was a fluttery, elderly lady. Yes, she had a room and supper and breakfast for two dollars. Ross looked at her ample proportions and smiled faintly; *she* liked her own cooking.

She showed him the room, and there was never a break in her chatter. It was a bare little room with a chipped, white-iron frame bed and a wooden washstand beside it. He interrupted her and said, "The room is fine, ma'am."

She smiled brightly at him and said, "Supper will be ready in half an hour."

He closed the door behind her, crossed to the single window, and looked out into a dusty backyard. He had the odd feeling that he was very exposed and abruptly jerked down the cracked green blind.

He poured water into the basin and washed his face and hands, then undid his bedroll and found a clean but wrinkled shirt. He laid out the belt-wrapped gun. Wearing it would not look out of place in this country.

He pulled Cleve's letter from his pocket and reread it. He had not wanted Cleve in on this hunt, but there had been no way of stopping him. Cleve wrote that he thought he had found the man, but he did not put a name to him. Ross frowned at the omission. But that would be corrected, when he saw Cleve, in a few days at the most.

He stared across the room, his eyes unseeing. His reserve was not a normal thing. It was born of two years of loneliness and a bitter, hardening resolution. He was going to kill a man—and perhaps a woman—if he ever caught up with them. Often, logic told him to abandon the search, to forget how his life had been shattered, and to try to make a new one. But the bitterness would not leave him, and the memories drove him on.

A man could not forget holding his first son in his arms, he could not forget watching the small daily changes in the baby, the first steps and the first words. He could not forget his plans for that son, the hopes for the future. He did not want her back—he had not wanted her back since the day she left. But he did want his son. Two years had passed; he wouldn't even know the baby. The thought drove him crazy.

Ross never put the title of wife or mother in place of the word "her." She was not his wife; she had not been since she ran away with Gary Anson. Not only had she taken Chris with her, but she had taken two thousand dollars of Ross's and Cleve's money—or rather the bank's money. They had borrowed it to buy that herd of short yearlings they had their eyes on. They had been forced to sell the ranch to make good the bank's loss. Cleve had said patiently, "The money's gone, Ross. The sooner we find them, the sooner we can get this over with and start rebuilding. It's sure as hell that two of us can cover more ground than one."

Sometimes the hopelessness of Ross's quest sickened him. In two years' time, he had searched the Territory of Arizona and most of California, asking his questions. Twice, he had been only a couple of days behind them, but some instinct had driven them on. He had thought they would seek the anonymity of a big city, but from the letter, Cleve was right. The richness of this new silver strike at Washoe was drawing people from all over the country. Virginia City was becoming as well known as the larger coastal cities, and the lure of quick and easy wealth might draw a man like Anson. Ross hoped Cleve was right.

He abruptly shook his head, putting away the old memories. He stood up as he heard Mrs. Wesley's voice calling him to supper.

He sat down to a meal of pot roast and browned potatoes and beans. The food was good, and she kept pressing more upon him. She never broke her flow of talk, neither asking nor wanting his opinion on anything. After half an hour of listening to her, he felt trapped, and the yearning to flee grew overwhelmingly. He had intended going to bed early, but he saw that she was settling down for a long evening of talk.

He stood up and interrupted her narrative of how selfish her neighbors were. He said, "You'll have to excuse me, ma'am. I've got to see someone."

The disappointment on her face did not deter him. He went to his room and strapped on the gunbelt. There was at least one man in this town who was interested in him. Until he learned what that interest was, it would not be wise to move about unarmed. He pulled the gun from its holster and dropped it back. It slid smoothly in the well-oiled leather.

He walked out quickly, then stood for a moment on the porch, letting his eyes adjust to the darkness. He touched the butt of the gun before he moved off the porch. There were two classes of life—the hunted and the hunters. Both had the same instincts and lived in the same atmosphere of listening and stealth. Tonight, he felt as though he were one of the hunted.

Folsom was a raw, little town, helped by the affluence of its distant neighbor. The people who passed through it on their way to and from Virginia City left some of their money here. The main street was crowded, and most of the stores were lighted, their doors open in invitation to anyone's dollar.

Ross moved on down the street. He wanted a drink and a quiet moment of reflection. He found a saloon, and the place belonged to any of fifty towns he had visited. Its furniture was crude and battered, the table tops scarred and burned. Sawdust covered the floor, and the room's air was heavy with the stale smell of sweat and liquor.

The tables were crowded, and he would have to stand at the bar. At one of the tables were the six women who had ridden the train from Sacramento. Two of them saw him, and their heads lifted, their eyes brightening with interest.

He did not respond to the look, and their interest faded. He found an empty space near the end of the bar and ordered his drink. The bartender poured the shot-glass full with a rush of liquid, looking as though he would overrun it. He cut off the flow at the exact instant, filling the glass to the brim.

Ross took the drink fast, and the whisky hit his stomach with powerful authority, its warmth rapidly spreading through his veins. He shook his head as the barkeep's hand moved toward the bottle.

The man to his right said, "Going to Virginia City?"

Ross tensed, then saw there was no personal interest in the question. The man was a good six inches shorter than he was, with stooped shoulders and a sagging belly that ballooned over his belt. His face was heavy with an inner weariness, pulling the eyes into a mournful droop. He turned to face Ross, and Ross saw the gleam of light from the badge he wore pinned to his shirt.

Ross said, "Yes," and the often asked questions poised on his tongue. A marshal remembered faces far better than most people.

"Lots of people rushing there," the marshal said. He turned his glass in his fingers as he shook his head. "And lots of them crawling back. I see them going and coming. I see so many faces I can't hardly remember my own."

That answered the questions Ross wanted to ask. He nodded in agreement and stared at his empty glass.

"Makes it tough on a man trying to do his job," the marshal said, complaint heavier in his voice. "The riffraff passes through here, looking for an easy dollar. Then the ones who go broke in Virginia City come back, and they're looking for a dollar. It makes it tough, all right."

Ross glanced at him again and saw the fear lying close behind his eyes, the fear that some incident would happen and the little security of his job would be gone.

A burst of laughter sounded from the women's table, and Ross turned his head. The man he had seen on the station platform and across the street at Mrs. Wesley's had joined the women, and they shrieked with laughter at something he said. The man did not look at Ross, but Ross knew he was there because of him. He showed a too-elaborate lack of interest in anything but the women, he tried to look like nothing but a man out for an evening, and he overplayed the part.

Ross said in a low aside, "Don't look now. Who's the man in the black shirt, sitting with those women?"

The marshal finished his drink, then slowly glanced about the room. His eyes rested only a fraction of a minute on the table, then came back to stare at the back-bar. His voice was low and shaky. "He's from Virginia City. Calls himself Tate. He was here a couple of months ago. Killed a man in a fight. Is he after you?"

Ross shrugged. He stayed with his elbows on the bar, staring into the mirror behind it. If Tate was after him, the marshal would be of little help. The table was at a wrong angle for Ross to get a full view of Tate, and people kept passing between it and the bar, blocking his vision. He got one brief glimpse of the man, his lips close to one of the women's ears, and he saw her turn her head to throw a full look at his back.

The skin was tight around Ross's jaw, and the tingle was racing along his veins. Whatever play Tate had in mind was forming fast.

Ross did not move until a hand touched his shoulder. He looked around, and one of the women stood behind him. He made a slight turn to his left.

"Come and join us, handsome," she said in a wheedling voice. Vestiges of beauty still remained behind the marks of hard wear. She was a boldly fash-ioned woman, her ample curves emphasized by the tightness of her dress.

The smile was tight on his lips as he shook his head. "Not tonight."

"Oh, come on," she insisted. Her hand reached out, and her fingers caressed his arm.

He saw Tate jump to his feet, his face black with rage. The man took three gliding steps, and stopped, an arm's length from Ross. "What the hell do you mean?" he yelled. His face mirrored rage, but his eyes were amused and filled with gloating. "If you think you can come in here and insult a lady."

The marshal edged away from Ross. He was treating this as a private quarrel. The woman said in a surprised bleat, "He didn't—"

"I'll take care of it," Tate said. His left arm swept out, brushing the woman aside. Nothing was between him and Ross. For a moment, there was the scrape of leather as men ducked out of line, then the room was deathly quiet.

It was nicely set up. Ross had not planned on the man's using one of the women. Seeing her behind him had led him into a bad mistake. He should have made a full turn from the bar; now, his right hand was in against it, and its hampering could be more than the margin.

He put bewilderment on his face and said, "Wait a minute, mister."

The burning satisfaction was more intense in Tate's eyes. This man liked to kill. It was stamped in those murky, hot depths. "Damn you," he snarled. "Don't try to talk yourself out of it."

Ross said in a shaky voice, "Listen. If it's an apology you want—" He gulped and swallowed hard. He had a deadly little man before him, but Tate was also making a mistake. He was delaying his action, enjoying the torment another man was going through.

Ross wiped his forehead again and raised his hand, a little as though to push back his hat.

"Beg, damn you," Tate said. "Beg—"

He broke off, and the startled yell, forming in his throat, never had time to sound. Ross whipped off his hat and slashed it at Tate's face. The sound of felt slapping flesh was loud and distinct.

Tate stumbled backward, his hand digging for his gun, but he was off balance and momentarily blinded. Ross had time to complete his turn, and his right hand was unhampered. His fingers closed about the butt of his gun, and it slid from the holster. He covered Tate before the little man could free his gun.

Ross snapped, "Hold it."

The words had no effect on Tate. A madness was in his eyes, and curses bubbled from his lips.

He screamed as he drew. His gun was swinging up when Ross fired. He fired at almost point-blank range, and he could not miss. The bullet took Tate in the chest, slamming him backward. He struggled to stay on his feet, but his treacherous knees insisted upon buckling. The gun was a tremendous weight, and try as he might, he could not raise it. His head dropped lower and lower, but the cursing never stopped. He took a step, his weight coming down hard, and his fingers opened, dropping the gun. He tried to throw himself forward as he fell, and the fingers of his left hand brushed Ross's vest and scraped down it. He lit on his face, then turned over on his side.

Silence held for a long moment, then one of the women screamed. It broke the silence, and talk babbled over the room. Ross had no ear for it. He bent over the figure on the floor and turned it on its back. Tate was dying. The light was fading from his eyes, and a creeping grayness was spreading over his face.

Ross asked, "Why did you want to kill me?"

The little man stared at him, and for an instant Ross thought he did not understand the question. Then Tate said huskily, "Go to hell." The words broke red bubbles at his lips. His eyes glazed, the breathing stopped.

Ross straightened and looked at the marshal. Pallor overrode the man's face, and he breathed hard.

"Well?" Ross asked in a challenging tone.

The marshal shook his head. "He asked for it. I thought he had you."

"I'm leaving tomorrow morning," Ross said flatly.

"Sure," the marshal agreed. "You won't be needed for the inquest." He said with an attempt at humor, "I can say it was a form of suicide."

Ross looked at the woman who had touched him. She was pressed tight against the bar, and the terror was just leaving her eyes. "Who was he?" he asked.

"I don't know." Her voice trembled. "I never saw him before he sat down at our table."

He seized her arm, and his fingers bit deep. "Don't lie to me."

She tried to jerk free and could not. "It's true. He bet me fifty dollars I couldn't get you to join us."

He stared long at her and decided she was telling the truth. He let go her arm and growled, "You lose. Pay him."

He moved toward the door, and men parted to give him passage. The silence was back in the room, and an awed respect was on those watching faces. He had seen that look before and did not like it. It set him too far apart from other men.

He looked back from the door. He could not see Tate; men were ringed about him. The marshal had said Tate came from Virginia City. If it was not a case of mistaken identity on Tate's part, it looked as though someone was fearful of Ross Stone's coming to Virginia City. Anson was the only man he knew who would be.

Chapter Three

HE AWAKENED in the morning, and last night's events came instantly into his mind. He shook his head as he climbed out of bed. He dressed and strapped on the gunbelt. Last night pointed to something, and from now on the gun would be a part of him.

He stepped out of the room, and Mrs. Wesley was waiting for him. She was literally bursting with her news. "There was another killing in town, last night," she panted. "And that worthless Ed Purvis stood by and let it happen." Her face clouded and she said darkly, "I'll bet he even helped in it."

Ross said in a wooden voice, "Maybe he couldn't do anything about it." He did not want to stay for breakfast. The meal would be an ordeal of listening to her.

Something in his manner aroused her suspicions. She looked at the gun on his hip, and the suspicion grew. "You said you had to see someone. You came here to kill him. You did it." She backed away, horror filling her face. "Get out of my house. You—you killer."

He did not like the word, though it was a truthful one. Explaining to her was useless. He thought she was going to scream, and he said in a harsh voice, "I'm leaving."

He walked back into his room and picked up the bedroll. He passed her without speaking.

He shouldered the bedroll and headed for the livery stable to purchase a horse. The man showed him a sorry collection of animals and asked an exorbitant price. Ross bit back his anger; the advantage of supply and demand was with the owner and there was not a damned thing he could do about it. He picked the least tired-looking of the lot and paid the price without comment.

He asked, "Can I leave him here until the train gets in?"

The livery stable attendant nodded. "Leave your

bedroll, too. If you're going to Virginia City, you're smart to go by horseback. Those stages beat a man to pieces. Good thing you bought early. I won't have a horse left tonight."

Ross had figured it the same way. He moved to the walk and sat down in a battered chair. He tilted it back against the building and pulled his hat low over his eyes. He had time to kill, and he let his thoughts aimlessly drift forward and back. He had been thinking that way ever since the roots of his life were destroyed. Cleve had argued that a man should put down new roots and forget the old, but Cleve was wrong. A man couldn't forget a son that easily.

He heard the chuffing of the train in the distance and pushed to his feet, not surprised that the hours had passed with so little effort. A lonely man grew practiced in the art of spending hours without outside help.

By the time he reached the station platform, the train had pulled to a stop. Its engine panted hard, like an old man after a forced walk. The platform was jammed with the crowding of two days' passengers, and Ross stood to one side, waiting for it to clear a little. At one end of the platform a short, fat man with a sweaty, beefy face yelled, "Bring your baggage along. If it ain't weighed, it don't go."

There were no manners in a crowd. Ross watched men shove ahead of women, trying to be first to the stages. He saw the six women of yesterday clustered in an isolated group. The one who had touched him looked lingeringly at him, and for a moment he

33

thought she was going to speak to him. He felt relief that she did not.

Six stages were backed up to the platform, and people were being loaded into them for the trip over the mountains. Even when the stages were uncomfortably full the agents insisted on pushing in another passenger. It was going to be a miserable trip for most of those people. If they thought they were tired and beaten after the train ride, wait until they reached Virginia City.

Only one woman still talked to the fat man, and Ross moved toward them. The fat man said irritably, "I told you you're allowed thirty pounds of baggage. Anything over is twenty-five cents a pound. Either pay for it or leave it."

The woman reluctantly counted three pieces of silver into his hand, sniffed at him, then moved hastily to a waiting stage.

Ross asked, "Do you know a man called Tate?"

The fat man's eyes were suspicious. "Why?"

It was likely that Tate had come in on horseback, but if he had a companion and had come by stage, Ross would like to know what could be waiting ahead of him on the trail.

He murmured, "I was just looking for him."

The suspicion in the eyes did not fade. "I ain't got time to be standing here answering questions every saddle tramp throws at me." He had sized up Ross well. This was no paying customer for the line.

He started to turn away, and Ross's hand flashed out and fastened onto the front of his shirt. The hand twisted, and the shirt tightened. The fat man squalled and struck at the hand, and Ross raked the knuckles of his left hand across the man's lips. The blow was not hard enough to break skin, but it carried a warning sting. He kept twisting the shirt, and the cloth tightened about the beefy throat until the fat man gasped for breath. Ross lifted him until the man's weight was balanced on his toes.

He said, "You're not as big a man as you think you are. And you've forgotten your manners."

The fat man stared into those cold eyes and said weakly, "No offense, mister. I don't know him."

Ross released him. "That's all you had to say."

As he turned away he saw two of the stage drivers glaring at him. The tat man worked for the same line as they did, and they would feel a certain loyalty. Several of the passengers stared wide-eyed out of the coaches. No doubt some of them had seen or heard about last night, and this incident would further mark him. He would move into Virginia City with a certain amount of notoriety, but it did not really matter.

The stages were pulling away, raising twin streaks of dust behind them. When all the coaches were in motion, the air would be gray with dust, and it would cling stickily to damp, sweating skin. There were rest stops along the route which would help a little, but each rest would only make the next leg of the trip more arduous.

He walked fifty yards down the street and passed an old and dilapidated buggy drawn up to the walk. A sorry horse was between the shafts, its head bent, its eyes patient and resigned. An elderly man sat in the seat, his head drooping almost as much as the ancient horse's. His eyes were closed, and his face was gray from sickness or exhaustion.

A woman stood on the far side of the buggy, trying to swing a heavy piece of luggage up into it. The luggage was as shabby as the buggy, and Ross saw the cord tied about it to keep it from flying to pieces. The woman swung it up, and Ross heard her pant for breath. She could not raise it high enough, for a corner caught the edge of the buggy, and the heavy article bounced back, almost tearing from her hands.

He stepped around the buggy and asked, "May I help, ma'am?"

He seized the baggage and effortlessly lifted it into the buggy. He straightened and looked into a pair of appraising eyes. He couldn't be sure of the color of those eyes; they would change shades with her moods. There was green in them, mixed with a blue or gray. He could be certain of one thing. He saw a coldness in them amounting almost to a dislike.

She was younger than he thought at first impression. She could have been on either side of twenty. Her face had a faint color, put there by her exertions with the luggage and the heat of the day. He saw good bone structure in the face, the flesh finely molded to it. It was a face that could turn many heads. The nose was cut on delicate but determined lines, and the same determined chiseling was in the jaw. The lips were soft and alive with mobility. She had a magnificent crown of hair with a glowing, coppery sheen. The coldness in her eyes nettled him, and he deliberately let his eyes drift lower. She had a figure to catch a man's breath, round where a woman should be round, the shoulders tapering into a tiny waist.

His appraisal overwhelmed hers, and she took her eyes away first and stared at the ground.

She said stiffly, "May I thank you?"

"Not if it hurts you," he drawled. It was odd the way personalities, completely strange to each other, could draw fire at the first contact. He was regretting the impulse that had prompted him to aid her. He had no interest in women now, and he never expected to have again. Burnt once, he would be crazy to stick his hand into the fire.

She was looking at him again, and that dislike had changed to anger, for her eyes were spitting sparks at him. There was no reason for her attitude, and it surprised him to find how it aroused anger in him.

He said, "It's surprising how little manners a man finds in this town."

She had the grace to turn a deeper color, but he saw the increased fire in her eyes.

"Did I ask you to stop?" she snapped. "Did I ask for your help?"

"What is it, Lynn?" the elderly man called from the seat of the buggy.

"Nothing, Father," she answered. "Nothing I can't handle myself."

Ross felt the hot impact of her eyes again. "You talk

about manners," she said scornfully. "Do you always use force to get your way?"

So she had seen that little incident with the fat man, and with a woman's perverseness she had reached a decision without learning the facts. She had only seen a big man manhandle a smaller one.

He touched his hat and said, "It's been a pleasure helping you."

She did not miss the sardonic tone, for as he moved past her he heard the quickened sound of her enraged breathing. The picture of her young freshness was very vivid before his eyes, and he resisted the impulse to look back. He heard the sound of the buggy wheels and still did not look around. She was forcing the old horse hard as she went by, and the wheels churned up large clouds of powdery dust around Ross. His lips twitched at the corners as he plodded through it. A hot-headed redhead. A dangerous combination for any man. His little flash of humor faded. He did not want any woman attracting him, and he admitted she had momentarily done so.

Chapter Four

ROSS tied his bedroll on behind the saddle and swung up.

The livery stable man said, "You're going to eat a lot of dust."

Ross had no doubt of it; all the stages were in front of him. He might not even catch the decrepit buggy.

At the outskirts of town one of the stages was halted. The driver was on the ground swearing as he put a wrench on a loosened hub nut. All Ross could see as he passed was the tremendous width of the man's shoulders and back and the remarkable reach of his arms. He moved on, and he was ahead of one of the stages. That would not last long, not with the six very excellent animals in the traces.

The road toward Henner's Pass was well marked by the slowly settling dust clouds raised by the passage of the stages. He looked down upon a sheer drop to his right and hastily steered the horse toward the inner side of the road. Those stage drivers had a great deal of raw nerve to whip their cumbersome spans and coaches around these tortuous turns.

It was better in the higher altitudes, for the breeze was much stronger, brooming the road clear of the choking dust. It was beautiful country here, near the top of the world. The green tips of the pine and fir and cedar were a vast multitude of spears thrusting toward the sky.

Ross rode in silence for a while, then turned his head as he thought he heard the rattle of wheels behind him. He heard the sound again and was sure of its origin, but a turn in the road blocked his vision. That should be the last stage out of Folsom, its driver pushing hard to make up some of the lost time.

The road wound sharply, limiting his view to a few yards before and behind him. He kept moving steadily forward, not trying to keep ahead of the stage. He was willing it pass him anytime it was ready.

He rode into a sharp bend and heard the sound of wheels again, this time lighter in volume and coming from ahead of him. That was probably the girl's buggy, and he was making better time than he thought to catch her here.

He came out of the curve and saw the buggy ahead of him. She was driving as hard as the old horse could take, and her father sat stiffly beside her. Both of them were too engrossed in watching the treacherous road to notice Ross's approach. He felt a surge of sympathy for her as he saw the rigid set of her shoulders. She was scared stiff, and well she might be on this road.

He was even with them before she was aware of his presence. He did not turn his head as he passed, but he felt her eyes upon him. He forced the horse harder; the horse was blowing hard from the pressure, but a hundred yards ahead, the road leveled out for a short distance. The animal could catch its breath there.

He had just reached the level area, when the sound of wheels behind him seemed louder. He looked around, and the heavy stage was rapidly overtaking the light buggy. The driver kept to the inside of the road, forcing the girl to the outer edge, and a yell of warning rose in Ross's throat.

It came out in a choked burst of sound as he saw the frightened girl move too far over. The road was wide enough for two vehicles to pass, but it would take cool nerves to hold steady while it was being done. At best, there would be only a few inches of clearance, and the bulky stage looming over the girl completely unnerved her. She sawed on the outer rein, pulling the horse still closer to the edge. The outer wheels of the buggy teetered on the road's edge, then suddenly slipped off into thin air. The inner wheels rose, and to Ross's horrified eyes everything seemed to be happening in slow motion. He saw the man hurl himself from the tilting buggy seat, but the girl was not going to get free. He jerked his horse around and spurred down the grade. He had a confused impression of the buggy flipping off into space, of a small figure hurtling through the air, and his throat was so tight his breathing made a rasping sound.

The stage driver had no intention of stopping. He stood up, lashing the teams to greater effort, and as Ross pounded by him he fixed that red beefy face and the tremendous width of the man in his mind. He would have no trouble in remembering him when he saw him again.

He threw off where the buggy went over, seeing that the man was already scrambling shakily to his feet. He looked over the side, and a tide of vertigo momentarily blinded him. His throat was dry and hot, and his stomach quaked and rolled. He briefly shut his eyes, then reopened them, He looked down into an almost sheer drop running into hundreds of feet.

A few stunted pines and bushes struggled for footholds in the craggy wall, and here and there a boulder perched precariously, looking as though the slightest breath of air would send it rolling and bouncing. A little stream tumbled down the bottom of the canyon, from this distance looking like a frothy ribbon of white.

He shook his head hard, then peered over the edge again. He caught a glimpse of color against a bush some dozen yards below him, and his heartbeat quickened. Behind him, he heard the man's voice raised in a weak and fearful call, but he did not look around. His eyes were not playing him tricks. That was a splash of color, and there was slight movement to it. How badly she was hurt he did not know, but she was conscious, and she had not fallen into the bottom of the canyon.

He yelled, "Hold on. Don't move. I'm coming."

He lowered himself over the edge, and his feet came alive with a new sensitivity as they felt for cracks and crevices. It was not a long descent, but it was a tortuous one. His fingers clung to tiny crevices until his boots tested each small outcropping. He would lower his weight a little at a time, his breath held against the sudden lurch that would mean the outcropping was giving away. The strain started in his shoulders and crawled the length of his arms. His legs grew shaky, and the sweat popped out in beads along his forehead, grew in volume, and ran together in small rivulets, stinging his eyes and itching his skin.

It seemed an eternity before he reached the bush. He panted hard, getting his breathing and words under control before he spoke. He cautiously tested the bush, and though it seemed firmly anchored, he was afraid their combined weight would tear it from its moorings.

He wiped his face with a trembling hand and said, "You all right?"

Her eyes held terror, but her face seemed composed enough. A branch or the rough scraping of a rock had torn a long, shallow scratch across her forehead. He saw the white outlines of her knuckles as she held onto the bush. He lifted his eyes to her face and asked again huskily, "Are you all right?"

It took a time for her to nod as though she had to debate the question from all sides. "I think so," she said finally.

His relief brought a grin to his face, softening its harsh outlines. She stared at it, surprise in her eyes, then slowly an answering smile reflected on her face.

He said, "We'll take it easy. We'll make it back okay."

A thought struck her, and she cried in dismay, "My father—"

"He's all right. He's up there on top, worrying about you."

A little stream of pebbles and dirt cascaded down near them, and he looked up and saw the man peering fearfully over the edge.

"See?" he said, pointing upward.

She lifted her eyes to the road's edge, and the sight of that familiar face erased all the tension in her. She said in a voice that was quite steady, "I'm ready."

He raised his voice in a yell. "Stand back. We're coming up." He wanted no dislodged earth and rocks hammering down at them from above.

He was wrong about all the tension being gone from

her; she only hid it well. He had to pry her fingers from their deathlike grip about the branch, and he kept talking in an even, soothing voice. Admiration grew strong within him. She was filled with terror, the rigidity of her fingers told him that, but he would never know it from looking at her eyes.

She went ahead of him, and he carefully guided her feet into the tiny niches and crevices. Once her foot slipped and slammed down onto his shoulder. The jar jolted through him and dislodged one boot. He wanted to yell with fear, and locked his teeth just in time to prevent the yell from slipping out. His fingers bit into their hold with new intensity, and his body was a rigid, straining line. Slowly, the dangling boot came back to the wall, groped cautiously about, and found its original place. He did not discover until later that his fingertips were raw and bleeding.

He paused until his breathing was steady and the panic willed out of him. He said, "All right," from an arid throat and started her upward again. It took a painful time for them to make the ascent, for he would not let her move until he was certain of the solidity of both of their grips and footholds. He was weak and trembling when he finally clambered over the edge. He walked several steps, letting the feel of the solid road erase the shakiness from his legs. He came back, and she was sitting on the ground, her head lowered. The man hovered over her, murmuring solicitious words.

She raised her head and looked at Ross, and again

there was only appraisal in her eyes. She said, "Once more I have you to thank."

He wondered what was running through her mind, why she apparently found those words so difficult to say. He stared at her, seeing the smooth, white expanse of her throat, the pulse beating hard at the base of it.

He turned his head and said gruffly, "I don't think that scratch is too bad."

When he looked at her again, she was on her feet, one hand touching her fingers to the red line across her forehead. She lowered her hand and looked at the faint stain on her fingers. She said in a wondering tone, "I didn't even know I was scratched."

He looked at her with remote eyes. There had been a moment of shared intimacy, but that was gone. "Are you all right?" he asked the gray-faced man. The man was trembling, but the reaction of fear and tension could be causing that. The knee of his trousers was torn out, but otherwise Ross could see no damage.

The man nodded without replying and placed one arm protectively around the girl's shoulders.

Ross moved to the edge of the road and looked down. He thought he could see the dark, shapeless blur of the buggy far below him, but because of the distance he could not be sure. The girl came to his side and stared into the depths.

She tried to laugh, and it came out in a shaky, broken sigh. "All our baggage is down there. And poor Nelly."

Ross said doubtfully, "It would be a mean climb down there to see about your things."

She shook her head. "You will not. I'm grateful enough for our lives." Worry wrinkled her forehead as she looked at the older man. "Though how I'm going to get Father to Virginia City, I don't know. He's been so sick."

Ross said, "I heard there're rest stations along the way. If we can reach one before dark, he'll be all right." He looked at the slanting rays of the sun. "Can he ride?"

He addressed the question to her, but the man answered. His tone was indignant. "I can ride. Lynn babies me more than necessary." He smiled at Ross and thrust out his hand. "If I haven't said my thanks before, it's not because I didn't feel them."

Ross nodded and clasped the hand. He could see the sincerity in the tired face, and an instinctive liking for this man sprang into life. "Forget it," he said. To take the abruptness from his words, he said, "I'm Ross Stone."

"Enoch Redford," the man answered. "And this is my daughter, Lynn."

A withdrawn quality was in her face as Ross nodded to her. She could build a wall faster than anyone he had ever known, and it gave him a queer, senseless irritation. He said harshly, "We'd better be moving, if we want to get off the road before dark."

He helped Redford into the saddle and turned to give the girl a hand up.

She shook her head. "I prefer to walk."

He did not miss her scrutiny of the horse, and she correctly evaluated the animal. A double burden might leave it a staggering wreck. His irritation grew. What did he care what kind of an appearance he made in her eyes? Still, he wished he had a better horse and trappings.

They plodded ahead of Redford, and Ross kept his stride short and slow. Each step here tore at the leg muscles, and the lungs labored and pounded, never quite getting enough air.

He watched her out of the corner of his eye. The dust film blotted out the fresh, young color in her face, and he saw the first drooping come into her mouth corners. Fatigue was mounting in her, but her head was still carried high.

He wanted to put his arm under her shoulders to bolster her step. It had been a long time since he had felt any tenderness toward a woman, and he put this present feeling down against the lonely months. He did not want the feeling; he would not let it grow, and he moved a step farther from her. He felt the force of her eyes upon him, and he kept his head turned from her.

It was almost dark when he spotted the rest station. "There it is," he said, pointing ahead of him.

Her laugh was shaky, but a laugh. "I'm glad. I don't know when I've been so tired."

He started to smile in response. She had spirit. Never once had she complained, and he knew how her muscles must be aching, for his own were setting up a dull protest. He drove the smile back and growled, "A hot supper and a bed, and you'll be all right." He looked at her, his face coldly wooden.

Her smile vanished, and her face turned as stiff as his. "And you will be rid of your burden," she said flatly.

He nodded. It was far better to smash any weakness now than let it grow into something that could hurt later.

The rest station was a crude rectangular log building with mud chinking. Before they reached it lamps were lit, their soft yellow light washing out through the opened door.

The last three stages to leave Folsom were lined up before the station. No teams were in the traces, so the passengers and drivers would spend the night here. His eyes were hard as he thought of that one particular driver. He had only a flash of the man's face to remember, but it was vividly stamped in his mind. That red, beefy face with its thick lips, the mouth open wide with its swearing and yelling.

He said awkwardly, "If you need—"

Her chin was high, her eyes direct and challenging. "If you are offering us money, Mr. Stone, don't. We have enough."

She stalked on ahead as soon as her father dismounted, and Ross watched them enter the station. His contact with her was broken, and he felt an odd sense of loss.

He found feed and water for the horse in the shed behind the larger building. The price was exorbitant and it would be that way from now on. Any supplies that came into this country had to be laboriously freighted over the mountains.

He heard the sounds of revelry coming from the station. He couldn't blame the passengers for trying to drown the memory of the trip behind them. Or perhaps it was the thought of the remaining part of the trip they were trying to wash away.

He could stand a drink himself, and he needed food. He started around the opposite corner of the station, and saw three men hunkered about a small fire. The fire splashed wavering light across their faces. One of them was the driver he wanted to find. The man said something to the other two, then threw back his head and burst into laughter.

The anger boiled up in Ross. It was not hard to recall the terror in the girl's eyes.

He started toward the group, and then noticed a woman coming around the opposite corner. He paused, wanting her to pass before he started anything. Not until the firelight touched her face did he recognize her. It was the woman who had approached him at the bar in Folsom.

Her face was intent on something, and she would have passed the group without pausing. The beefy driver did not let her. He jumped to his feet and seized her arm. "What's your hurry, sweetheart?"

The older man looked disgusted, but the younger one was grinning. "Go to it, Mack," he said.

The woman snapped, "Let go of me." Her voice showed no fear, only scorn. "You're wasting your time. You haven't got enough money to buy thirty seconds of my time."

Mack's laugh was coarse and jarring. He drew her close, and she struck at him. His upflung arm blocked the blow. "I've got something better than money for you." He pinned her arms, and his weight bent her backwards.

Ross moved to them. He seized Mack's shoulder and jerked him back a step. "You heard her," he snapped. "Let her go." He did not care what started this fight; he only wanted it started.

Mack turned a startled face, then it went black with anger. "Why, damn you—"

Ross hit him before the sentence was complete. He drove a hard set of knuckles into the thick mouth and the force of the blow shocked Mack back. His face looked stunned, and blood spurted from split lips. He smeared a hand across them, crimsoning the lower half of his face. An enraged bellow burst past his lips as he sprang forward. Ross set himself to meet the charge. He was taller than Mack, but Mack had a body like a pine log and thick, muscular legs drove him forward. He had the advantage in weight and in breadth of shoulders.

"I'll knock your damned head off," Mack yelled and threw a wild fist.

Ross jerked his head aside, feeling the breath of the fist as it grazed his cheek. He had power in front of him, raw, animal power that would take considerable battering before it was sapped. He doubted a few punches would send Mack down and keep him there, and he set about wearing him down.

He put a fist under the breast bone, drawing a harsh grunt out of Mack. He pumped two blows into the face, feeling flesh flatten under his knuckles. Mack kept boring in, his swearing coming between grunting gasps for breath. The ferocity of his wild blows never diminished. Ross slipped those blows or took them on defensive forearms. He was right in his evaluation. Mack had power but little skill to enforce it. The knowledge made Ross a little careless. He slipped aside from one fist, but another took him a glancing blow just above the left eye. It was like being hit with a club. It rang bells in his head and put water in his eyes. It broke him backward, and momentarily his arms were weakened and drooping. Mack sprang at him with a triumphant bellow.

Two huge arms clamped about Ross's chest, the hands locking together in the small of his back. Mack's hard head was pressed tight under Ross's chin, and the pressure started. It was bad from the start, and it grew steadily worse. After a few seconds of it Ross gasped for breath, and the forehead pressed against his throat made breathing even more difficult. His eyes began to swim, and red lights burst before them, red lights that exploded into black blotches.

The growth of the blackness brought on a momentary panic, and he expended his strength in a useless thrashing around. His arms were pinioned, but he could twist and jerk his trunk and kick and thresh his legs.

The blackness was almost solid after the exertion. His lungs were filled with fire instead of air, and his throat felt raw where Mack's stiff, bristly hair ground into it. Mack's grip never weakened. His hands, digging into Ross's back, felt as though they would snap his spine.

Suddenly Ross went limp in that viselike grip, sagging toward the ground, and he heard the satisfied grunt in Mack's throat. Some of that awesome power gripping his body slackened, and he called upon the remnants of his fading strength. He spent them in one final surge, springing backward against Mack's loosening hands. The hands clawed frantically for a renewed hold, but Mack's reflexes were an instant too late. Ross was free and backing away. Mack pursued him, his mouth twisted with his swearing, and Ross forced more speed into his wobbly legs. He backed in a circle, beating at the hands that reached for him. One of them fastened on his shirt, and he slashed at it with the edge of a palm. He knocked the hand free, hearing the ripping of his shirt.

Strength flowed back with each gulp of fresh air. His legs were steadier, and his eyes were clearing. Mack's frantic clawing now no longer even touched him.

Mack stopped and growled in helpless frustration, "God damn you. Stand still."

Ross stared bleakly at him. He was tired, but his arms and legs responded to his demands. He still gasped for breath, but the searing fire was gone from his lungs. A crowd had gathered, drawn by the noise, and more people were streaming around the corner of the station. He caught a glimpse of the woman's face, and it was set in fixed fascination.

He said, "All right, Mack," and glided forward. He made sure those pawing hands did not fasten upon him again. He had made one mistake, and its cost was almost more than he could pay. He would not make it again.

He threw his fists with sharp, stinging effect into Mack's face; in a few moments he had the face cut to pieces. The blood from a dozen cuts mingled and dropped in a red curtain. Mack's movements became vague and uncertain, and each breath formed and broke a red bubble at his lips.

Ross still threw his punches from long range, knowing it was not yet time to move in close. One taste of the power of those arms was enough.

Mack rushed him, his pain and anger forcing him into a blind, senseless charge. He tripped over his own feet and went down. He sat staring stupidly about him, his face a dripping, bloody mess.

"Get up," Ross said. "I want you to remember this for a long time."

He heard a sharp gasp and jerked his head around. Lynn stood at the fringe of the crowd, her face white, her eyes fixed in appalled fascination on the bloody ruin of Mack's face. She looked back at Ross, and there was a dawning terror in her eyes. She covered her face with her hands and fled. Ross's mouth was a hard, bitter line as he watched her leave. The look on her face was more expressive than any words.

Mack was having a hard time climbing to his feet. A knee buckled, throwing him back to the ground, and when he finally straightened, he reeled in wobbly circles.

Ross moved in on him. The power in those arms was almost dissipated, and Mack spent great effort in trying to lift them above his waist. Ross had intended further punishment for the man, but the look on the girl's face changed that. Now, he wanted this over with as quickly as possible. He speared a left hand into Mack's mouth, his knuckles slipping against those broken lips. He hit the man a dozen times, and blood splattered under each of them. It took all of them to put Mack down. A tired sigh slipped past Mack's lips, he rocked back and forth, then slowly he fell apart and pitched forward on his face. He jerked a little, then he was still.

Chapter Five

R oss glared at the crowd, and it retreated before the wildness in his eyes. He stared at Mack's two companions and saw murderous hatred in the younger man's face. His fists were still balled. Ross locked eyes with him, and the man looked away. He looked at the older man and saw no hatred in his eyes, only a calm weighing. Neither was going to pick this up, and he was relieved, for weariness dropped upon him with crushing weight. His legs felt limp as string, and he wanted to sit down. He began to feel all the blows; each had a clamoring voice, and joined together they set up a chorus of aches and pains.

He took a few steps, thrusting hard with each heel to brace his legs against their shakiness. He looked back, and the younger man had dropped on his knees beside Mack. He lifted Mack's head, and Mack groaned. I hope he hurts, Ross thought savagely. I hope he hurts worse than I do. He moved on a staggering course toward the horse trough near the shed.

He stopped at the trough and turned his head. A few people had followed him out of curiosity, and he stared at them with hard, unfriendly eyes. They retreated hastily.

He looked at his shirt, whose front was stiff with blood, both his and Mack's. There was a long rip in it where Mack's hands had fastened, and Ross grimaced with distaste. He stripped off his shirt, and thrust his face into the water of the trough. It was cold and stinging against bruised, cut flesh. He held it there, blowing hard against the water. He felt better when he raised his head. The water had a reviving force, driving the foggy haze out of his mind.

He soaked the ruined shirt in the trough, but before he could use it, the woman said, "Let me do that."

He turned his head and scowled at her painted face. So she had not left with the rest of them. She ignored his scowl and took the shirt from him. He was too tired to argue with anyone.

She said softly, "Thanks."

His puzzled frown disappeared as he realized she thought he had jumped Mack because of her. He did not have the energy to explain.

Her hands were gentle and sure as she bathed his face and chest. "You're big," she said, admiration in her voice.

He grinned. Tired and beaten, he appreciated any kindness.

The grin touched something in her, for she averted her face and said, "Don't laugh at me. I owe you this much for what you did for me tonight. And for what I almost did to you in Folsom."

He sensed an underlying longing under that hard shell and said, "I'm not laughing at you. Can't a man look as if he feels better?"

Her eyes flicked across his face, and she said, "Sure," in a voice that was not quite steady. She dropped the cloth to the ground and asked, "Do you have another shirt?"

"It's in my bedroll in the shed." He told her where to find it and waited.

She came back with the shirt and said, "This is your last one." She unbuttoned it and shook out the wrinkles.

She helped him slip into it, then buttoned it. As her fingers worked she looked up at him. "I'm Ida. If you're in Virginia City, look me up."

"I might do that," he said uncomfortably. He pushed her hands away as she reached for the tails of his shirt. "I can do that." He turned from her, unbuckled his belt and thrust the shirt inside his pants. The instinctive gesture put a smile back on her face.

She had an appeal to a lonely, tired man, and he fought away its touch. He said, "Thanks," and hesitated. He looked over her shoulder, and what else he had in mind to say was wiped away.

Lynn stood at the corner of the building. The revulsion was gone from her face, but it was cold and unfriendly. How long had she been there, how much of the incident had she seen, and what inference did she draw from it? Ross swore at himself for the questions. What difference did it make?

Ida turned her head and saw Lynn. "Ah," she said softly, and the word could have meant anything.

Lynn whirled and disappeared. There was a knowing brightness in Ida's eyes, when she looked back at Ross. She ran her hand through her yellow hair. "You wouldn't believe it, but this used to be red. There's something about red hair that gets a man." She smiled mockingly at the increasing anger in his eyes. "Remember what I said about looking me up." She flipped her hand at him and left.

Ross's anger faded into a reluctant grin. A man was always pleased when he appealed to a woman. And he had. He could feel it in every touch of her hands.

He felt in his pockets for the makings. He rolled and lit his cigarette. The smoke burned against his cut mouth, but it tasted good. He hunkered on his heels, staring moodily into the darkness.

He did not know the man was near until the voice

said, "Never thought I'd see Mack whipped."

He lifted his head and looked into the face of the older of Mack's companions.

"Took a good man to do it," the man said. Firelight reflected from his eyes, showing the friendly twinkle in them. "I'm Welles Overhill." He squatted down beside Ross. "Drive one of the stages. And I'm no friend of Mack's. Don't like to see a big man use his weight like he does. Some of the younger drivers think he's cock of the heap. They didn't think he could be whipped. Like me." He grinned. "You'll be a marked man. Lots of people will remember tonight."

Yes, Ross agreed silently. Including a girl. Despite himself, his thoughts kept slipping back to her.

He said flatly, "He forced a girl's buggy off the road, trying to pass her. He never even stopped to see what help he could give."

Overhill nodded. "That's Mack. He's been earning that beating for a long time. He's got to be tops in everything he does. He's got to drive faster than anybody else, he's got to be harder and tougher than the next man. You'll see him again, if you stay around Virginia City—" He hesitated, and Ross realized he was waiting for a name.

"Ross Stone," he said. He watched the eyes. It was just another name to Overhill.

Overhill nodded. His face turned shrewd. "That girl standing off by herself and watching the fight—she the one he forced off?"

He chuckled at Ross's expression. It gave him his

answer. "You're kinda sore at her for the way she took it."

Ross's growl did not form a word, and Overhill laughed again. "If she didn't know what the fight was over, it was a kinda brutal thing for her to see."

Ross snapped, "I'm not interested."

The chuckle did not sound again, but Ross felt it was there. "Lots of traffic going over this road," Overhill said. "Everything rushing to Virginia City to get their hands on some of that silver." He was silent, and Ross could feel more questions forming in the man's mind. "You don't look like the type that's going there."

"No," Ross said and straightened. His belly grumbled, and he remembered how long it had been since he had eaten. "Join me for supper."

Overhill shook his head. "Already ate." He stood up and beat the dust out of his pants: "You watch Mack. He won't let tonight stop where it is."

Ross took a step, then stopped. He did not know how the Redfords were fixed. He did not want to be burdened with them the remainder of the trip, but he could not leave them stranded here.

He asked what the fare for two was to Virginia City and fished out the amount Overhill named. "That girl you saw with her father." His tone invited no comment. "Can you take them on in?"

The twinkle in Overhill's eyes was deeper, but he accepted the money without speaking.

Ross started to say something, then bit off the words. He nodded abruptly and walked away. The sooner he forgot Lynn Redford, the better off he would be. . . .

He had his choice of beans for supper and badly cooked beans at that. He ate stolidly, aware of the covert glances passengers gave him. Overhill was right about one thing. Ross Stone was a marked man, at least where this group of people was concerned.

Chapter Six

R OSS was awake with the first strong light of day. He pitched the saddle into place and kicked the air out of the horse's belly before he tightened the cinch. The animal made a blubbery, dismal snort of acceptance of this early-morning ride, then stood with drooping head.

Ross swung into the saddle and put a final look on the station. This early departure meant he would miss breakfast. The memory of last night's supper of scorched beans did not make the miss too hard to bear.

The road took a downward plunge toward the American River crossing. Although he had never traveled this route before, he had asked enough questions about it to know where he was. Glenbrook Station at Lake Tahoe lay ahead. From there, he had been told he could see Carson City. An hour's moderate travel from there should bring him to Virginia City.

He had an early enough start that none of the stages overtook him. He pressed on through Carson City, ignoring the protests of his empty belly. He would wait and eat with Cleve in Virginia City. He pushed the old horse hard during the last part of the trip, trying to cut minutes off of that final hour. Its head was sagging lower than usual when he reached Virginia City.

The traffic on the streets astounded him. They were packed with horsemen, pedestrians, and wagons. Ross utilized the slowness of the pace to observe this newest of the fabulous mining camps. He passed the open doors of saloons and did not see how it was possible to get another customer inside, and still men tried to shove through the doors. Restaurants and hotels were filled to overflowing. Clothing stores offered their wares on placards in the windows, and the prices made him wince. He rode by the Wells Fargo station, and the platform before it was heaped high with goods and packages. Shipping always indicated the growth of a city. By the volume Wells Fargo was handling, Virginia City was bursting its seams.

He saw a livery stable ahead and edged his horse toward it. He could make better time on foot than on horseback.

The livery attendant spat an amber stream into the dust and asked, "How long you staying?"

Ross shook his head and said, "I don't know." It depended upon how right Cleve was, how long it took to end the search, how long his small supply of money lasted.

The hostler grinned. "Bucking this country decides for most. It takes some a week, some a month, and some stick."

Ross said noncommittally, "I don't know which

class I belong in. Can I pick up my bedroll later?" The man nodded, and Ross turned the horse over to him. "Treat him kindly," he said. "He deserves it."

He moved through the stable's wide entrance and joined the throng on the walk before it. He was jostled and pushed by men dressed in suits of the finest broadcloth and immaculate white linen shirts. They in turn were shouldered ahead by men in rough red and blue flannel shirts, their boots mud-caked, their hands dirty and horny from toil in the mines. Now and then a half-starved-looking Paiute or Washoe Indian tottered along the curb with a heavy load of fagots on his back.

Mountains surrounded the city, their slopes still streaked with snow. Mounds of freshly turned dirt dotted those slopes like anthills. Men dug frantically into the soil, trying to wrest the earth's riches from it, and it impassively resisted them, defeating most of\ them in the end.

Tons of ore were piled in heaps along the curbstone, and heavy ore wagons were constantly bringing more into the city. Every store and office offered for purchase the sale of feet. It looked as though there were three assay offices to every other kind of business, and most of them were housed in tents. He looked into the open entrance of one tent and saw a small furnace, half a dozen crucibles, a bottle of acid, and a hammer. The assayer was a ragged man with a heavy growth of beard, his face showing lean and hungry above it.

He caught Ross's interest and stepped hastily outside. His eagerness showed in the trembling of his hand on Ross's arm.

"I can sell you twenty feet for twenty dollars, stranger," he said. "Every foot is worth a thousand."

Ross shook off the clutch of the clawlike hand. "Friend," he drawled. "You look like you need those riches worse than I do." He moved on down the walk, grinning mirthlessly at the incident. That was one of Virginia City's carrion birds, waiting to strip any luckless or unwary stranger.

He stopped at the street crossing and glanced about him. Damn Cleve for not writing his address. Where would he start to look for him? The hotels would be the logical starting point, but his immediate need was a meal. He saw a tent ahead with a crudely lettered sign reading "Restaurant" hanging over it. He made his way to it, and a dozen feet from it, the heavy smell of stale cooking wrapped itself about him.

He had to wait several minutes before there was room for him to step inside. A crude counter ran the width of the tent. There were no tables or chairs. Men stood at the counter and wolfed down their food. Eating was a necessity here, not a pleasure. The smell was worse inside, and the grease spitting and popping on the hot iron stove added to it.

Ross waited until an empty space showed at the counter, then stepped to it.

The cook said, "You got your choice of pork and beans and fried potatoes, mister."

Ross nodded, and the cook ladled beans out of a

grimy, battered pan and scraped potatoes from their bath of grease in a huge frying pan. He poured soot-black coffee into a dented tin cup without a handle.

Ross ate with no expression on his face. The beans were burned and the potatoes soggy, and the coffee tasted as though the grounds were days old.

He paid a dollar and a half for the meal and was relieved to get out of the reeking, fetid air of the restaurant. He let the traffic on the walk carry him along for a while, breasting it only when he came to a hotel. He patiently worked from one to another until he was sure he had covered every one in the city. The frown was deep on his face as he left the last one. He threw off the first little thrust of fear. As crowded as the hotels were, it was likely Cleve had found lodgings with some individual. At the last hotels Ross asked for space for himself, and one of the clerks told him he might find something at the Palace.

It was late when he walked out onto the street again, and the wear of the day was pulling at him. The saloons were ablaze with lights, but the rest of the town was darkening. He reluctantly gave up his search for the night.

He saw the Palace bar across the street. One section of its window was broken, and the last three letters of the word Palace were gone. The sound of raucous laughter increased as he approached the place, and a woman's shrill voice rang out over the tinny sound of a piano. The clerk must be wrong. The Palace sold liquor, not sleeping space.

· · ·

As long as he was this close he stepped inside and asked the bartender. The man jerked his head toward a room at the back. "You're kinda late," he said. "But they might squeeze you in." His face was sympathetic. "It's hell finding a place to sleep in this town."

Ross knew a growing dismay as he looked in on the room. Twenty men slept on the floor, so crowded together that if a man flung out his arm in his sleep, it would land across the body of the man next to him. The attendant in charge said, "I got one place left, mister. It'll cost you three dollars." His tone said take it or leave it.

Ross's weariness and need for sleep won over the other considerations. He paid the three dollars and gingerly stepped over sleeping bodies to a cramped space near the far wall. It had the lone advantage of not being completely surrounded by flesh, but the wall was a sounding board against which all the noise from the saloon rebounded.

He stretched out on the floor and lay there staring at the ceiling. He wished he could have found Cleve. He thought of Lynn Redford and her father and hoped that they had found better accommodations. He fell asleep, thinking about them.

Chapter Seven

ZACHARY TANNER paced about the office, his nervousness showing in the jerkiness of his stride. Where in the hell was Tate? He had expected him back by this afternoon at the latest. Had something gone wrong, had Tate missed Stone in Folsom? He cursed himself for the worried questions that kept bubbling up into his mind. He did not have the exact date. It might be a week or even more before Stone arrived. Tate would simply wait in Folsom until Stone came. It was foolish to torture himself by useless speculation.

He moved to the window and stared out at the teeming traffic of Virginia City's main street. Was Ross Stone one of that sea of humanity flowing beneath his window? Would a face turn his way, stare incredulously, then yell as it recognized him?

He looked at his trembling hands and slammed them hard against the window sill. Who would recognize Zachary Tanner as a man called Gary Anson two years ago? He was twenty-five pounds heavier, and his face was covered with a full beard and mustache. His own mother would have difficulty recognizing him now. He clenched his fists. Just as he was beginning to believe the nightmare of that long flight was over, it started again. There was no doubt Stone had picked up the trail again. Hadn't he sent his brother ahead of him? How many more were working with Ross Stone?

It didn't make any difference how many of them

there were; it didn't make any difference if Stone himself reached Virginia City. He was through running. He glared out at the traffic and said, "I got your brother. I'll get you the same way."

The words gave him assurance, and his face brightened. Stone's brother had not been sure who Zachary Tanner was until the last moment. Stone could be as much in the dark. He was up against a different man now, affluent and powerful.

Tanner held out his hands, and they were quite steady. His face was cold and hard. He had let momentary panic touch him, and it would not happen again. He had come here almost broke, and in six months he had whipped this city. He owned this saloon, the stage-line that ran between Folsom and Virginia City, and half a dozen pieces of valuable mining property. There was more to be had for the plucking. Give him another six months, and he could own the city.

He looked at his clothes, his expensive boots. There were months of privation behind the getting of them, behind his rise to his present position, and Stone would never take any of it away from him.

He thought back over his meetings with Stone. There had been only two of them, both brief and of no particular importance to Stone. Valerie, however, had talked so much about Stone that he knew every physical characteristic of the man.

Valerie was the danger. Stone would remember her, and she could lead him to Zachary Tanner. There was always the danger that Stone might see Valerie on the streets. Tanner took another rapid turn around the room. Should he send her out of the city? He shook his head; he was not going to be pushed into any panicky action. If Stone by some miracle got past Tate in Folsom, it still did not mean that he would see Valerie. He could order her to stay in the house until he could make other arrangements.

Let Stone come to Virginia City. What could a lone man do against the power Tanner had built here? He could not quite still the chilly voice inside his brain. It whispered, Remember his ability with a gun?

He stepped to the door and jerked it open. Mack should be back by now. Mack might have seen Tate in Folsom. He might know if anything had happened there.

He yelled at a man lounging in the hallway, "Jude, find Mack. Tell him I want to see him."

Something must have showed in his voice, for Jude had a curious look.

"God damn it," Tanner shouted. "Move."

Jude said, "Sure, Zach," and went down the hall with rapid strides.

Tanner shut the door and touched his forehead. It was damp again. But most of his composure was restored. Jude's alacrity did that. He had men like Jude and Mack and a half dozen others, men who would obey his slightest order. And they did it out of fear of him.

He sat down at his desk and lit a cigar. The smoke tasted better this time. His face was cold and hard as he waited for Mack.

His jaw dropped as Mack came into the room. Mack

moved haltingly and painfully, and his face was battered beyond belief. A frown set on Tanner's face. Damn Mack and his reckless driving! He must have sent a stage over the side; he had to, to look like that.

The cigar bobbed angrily in the corner of his mouth as he talked. "Mack, if you've wrecked a stage, you'll pay for it."

"I didn't wreck no stage," Mack said sullenly.

Tanner's eyes widened at the thought that Mack had been in a fight. But that couldn't be. No man could give Mack that much of a beating. Tanner had seen him in action too many times.

"What happened?" he asked.

"Nothing." The sullenness was more pronounced in Mack's voice.

Tanner waited and saw that Mack was not going to talk. He impatiently dismissed the matter. They were Mack's hurts, not his.

"Mack, did you see Tate in Folsom?"

"No," Mack snapped. A wicked fire glowed in his eyes. He was nursing a hatred against someone or something. He closed a big hand and winced. The movement was painful. "You ain't going to see him, either. Anyplace," he said.

The renewed fear was a clammy hand tightening around Tanner's throat. He asked in a husky voice, "What do you mean?"

Mack licked his lips. He enjoyed what he had to say. Not because Tanner was involved, but because he hated Tate like poison. Tate was contemptuous of the big man and showed it. Mack licked his lips again and said, "He's dead. The little bastard tried to gun someone in Folsom. I talked to some of the passengers who seen it. They said this big guy shot Tate before Tate more than thought about pulling his gun."

"Who was this big man?" Tanner's words came out spaced poorly.

Mack cursed viciously. "I never saw the son of a bitch before he jumped me at the station."

"Alt," Tanner said. The same man who had killed Tate had beaten Mack, and both of them were experts in their fields. Even if Mack could not put a name to the man, Tanner had no doubt it was Stone. Mack said the fight had occurred at a station. Did he mean one of the way stations enroute here, or the station in Folsom? He silently cursed a dead man and his letter, then felt a queer kind of resignation.

He said in a low voice, "Describe him."

Mack exaggerated Stone's size, but he had the coloring and the scar down pat. His eyes sharpened. "Do you know him?"

Tanner glanced at his hands. "Never heard of him before," he said. He studied Mack, seeing for the first time the hurt the whipping had administered to his spirit. The big man had one thing on which to rely— his brute power over other men. That had been taken from him, and the thought goaded and lashed him.

Tanner put amusement into his voice as he said, "He whipped you good, didn't he Mack? I never thought I'd see that happen."

70

Mack's eyes were insane with anger. "Damn you. Shut up." He leaned over the desk, his hands opening and closing.

"Mack." The name was coldly authorative, and it checked the murderous rage in Mack's eyes.

Tanner said soothingly, "Mack, it's no disgrace to be whipped. Every man runs into a better one now and then."

Mack's face was livid, the color obscuring the bruises and cuts, "I'll be damned, if he's a better man. I'll find him again. When I do—" He broke off and looked at his clenched hands. He raised and shook them in Tanner's face. They looked huge and mis-shapen, with the black, bristly hair reaching to the second joint of his fingers. "He'll be damned sorry he ever saw me," he said thickly.

Tanner shook his head, and there was pity in the gesture. "I admire your courage, Mack, but you're crazy. Look what he's already done to you. My advice is to stay away from him. I don't want anything happening to you."

Mack's chest swelled. "I'll show you," he shouted. "I'm looking for him now. Some of the boys are keeping an eye out for him. Let him come here."

"He whipped you once," Tanner said softly. The tool was honed to a razor's sharpness. It was time to use it. "I'm betting five hundred he can do it again."

Mack loved money. Five hundred was an enormous sum to him. He was too far gone in his anger to even question Tanner's interest in this. "I'll take that bet," he said savagely. "But there ain't going to be just a whipping this time. I'm going to kill him." He turned and rushed from the room in a rage.

Tanner murmured, "Stone, you'll be up against a different kind of odds now." Even without anger to spur him on, Mack was a brute of a man. A month ago, Tanner had seen him kick a man to death. But the beating he had suffered would instill an animal cunning in him. Tanner was guessing that the first fight was a fair one. Mack would not make that mistake again.

He stood up and crossed the room, hesitated, then turned abruptly back to the desk. He opened a drawer and lifted out a gun. He studied it for a moment before he tucked it in the waistband of his trousers. Ordinarily he never wore one. He paid men to do that for him, but Ross Stone was out there somewhere.

He went through the crowded main room of the saloon, not noticing the nods and greetings given him. Susie tried to stop him near the door, and he roughly knocked aside her hand. "Damn it," he snarled. "I'm busy."

He drew several deep breaths as he stepped out onto the walk. It was near midnight, but the street was crowded. He moved north with the flow of the crowd, forcing his eyes straight ahead. It was temptation to look around, to scan the faces behind and to each side of him. Stone could so easily be one of those faces.

As he approached the Nevada House a tall man was just descending its steps. Light from the lobby bathed a short segment of the walk, and Tanner sucked in his breath. God, it was Stone. There was no mistaking him.

Stone stood on the bottom step, looking about him in evident indecision. Tanner was twenty feet away, and he was going to have to pass him. He wanted to grab his gun but he kept his hand rigidly away from the tails of his coat. His stride was even and unhurried. He must do nothing to draw the slightest amount of unusual attention to himself.

He let his eyes touch Stone as he passed him, the normal glance one passer-by would give another. From the corner of his eye he saw that Stone watched him. Was it only a casual glance, or was there growing recognition in his face? He wished he dared look at him longer, but he had passed him.

He moved to the head of the block before he dared stop. He looked in both directions, turning slowly as a man might do who had changed his mind about his errand. His hand was under his coat, the fingers touching the butt of the gun. If Stone had followed him, the element of surprise would be his before Stone was fully sure who it was.

He completed the turn and expelled his breath in a long sigh. Stone was walking in the opposite direction, his height outstanding among the other men on the walk.

Tanner's eyes were fired with an exultant glow. Stone had not recognized him. At least for the moment he was safe. He quickened his stride toward the house two blocks away.

He stopped and stared at it before he entered it. It was one of the most substantial houses in Virginia City, and he felt pride each time he saw it. This was another of the things Stone would not take from him.

He unlocked the door and stepped into the parlor. He crossed the room to the edge of light coming from the bedroom door. He paused with his hand on the knob, his breath quickening. He had known this woman for two years, and she still had the power to put a stir in his blood. He knew before he opened the door he would find her before a mirror. Her endless vanity amused him, but it was not unfounded. A beautiful woman should be proud and work at it.

He eased open the door, and he was right. She sat before a dressing-table mirror, absorbed in the work of powdering her shoulders. She was dressed in nothing but a filmy blue wrapper, and through the sheer material he could see the white of her skin. He had ordered that wrapper for her from San Francisco, and it had arrived only a week ago. He took pleasure in dressing Valerie's beautiful body.

The wrapper was down from her shoulders, and his eyes rested on the lovely line of her shoulders and the smooth flow of her neck into them. He entered the room and moved a step to one side. He could see her reflection in the mirror, and her breasts were almost entirely exposed. The drums were beginning to throb in his blood again.

She was too intent on her work, and yet he knew that she was aware of him. He had no doubt she had heard his key in the lock and had set up this tableau. A sound-less chuckle swelled inside him. Even though he knew her devices he appreciated them. She was a clever woman and always kept his interest fresh and new.

He moved to her and took the powder puff from her hand. "Let me do that."

"Oh," she gasped. "I didn't hear you come in." There was only laughter in her eyes.

He loosened the wrapper, and it fell about her hips. He dusted the powder on her shoulders, her throat and on her breasts. She was a full-bodied woman, made for pleasure, and his hand was not quite steady.

He frowned at the part in her hair. The hair at the roots there showed its normal blonde color. She was careless about keeping it retouched. He stared at her reflection in the mirror, seeing the tiny scar where the mole had been. She was a baby about pain, and she had protested long about having the mole burned off. With her hair now black and the mole gone, would Stone recognize her? But her features were the same, and when a man knew a woman as well as a man knew his wife, some mannerism or gesture could always recall her. No, he must keep her in the house until Stone was gone.

He asked, "Chris asleep?" and she nodded. He knew mixed emotions about the boy. There were times when he felt a great affection for him, then at others the sight of the boy brought back forcefully the thought that Stone was hunting them. He would have left the boy long ago, but she would not have it.

She was watching him with a shining expectancy in her eyes, and he said, "Valerie," in a husky voice. Her lips were full and red, and her long, narrow eyes had the suggestion of a slant, giving her an Oriental look that aroused interest in every man who saw he.

Her fingers dug into his neck and shoulders. Those restless, working fingers seemed to dig deep inside him, trying to reach the very core of his vitality.

His arms tightened about her, and he savagely kissed her. They had an animal need of each other, a need that was constantly being drained, then replenished.

He lifted his head and looked at her. Her eyes were closed, her lips slightly parted.

"Gary," she said with a little moan. Her hands pulled at his head, trying to bring it back to her.

The name was like a dipperful of ice water full in the face. She was the only person in Virginia City who knew him by that name, and he had repeatedly warned her never to use it. The sound of it swept away the heat in his blood. It brought back the fact that Stone was here in Virginia City.

He pulled back from her, lifted his hand, and slapped her. Her eyes flew open, and she stared at him. The wrapper fell to the floor, but neither of them was aware of it. She stared at him wide-eyed, the outlines of his fingers standing out in bold relief on her cheek. She raised an incredulous hand and touched the hurt, and her eyes were dazed with disbelief.

"Why?" she whimpered. "Why, Gary?"

His face was a mask of fury, and his fingers bit cruelly into her collarbone. "Goddamn it," he shouted. "I told you that name was gone. I told you never to use it."

His fear and rage blended into a great black cloud. At the moment, he could have killed her and known no loss.

"You're hurting me," she moaned. "I forgot—" She almost said the name again, then hastily changed it to Zachary. "Does it make any difference here?" she pleaded.

His fingers dug deeper. "You forget and use it here, and you'll forget and use it somewhere else." His hands were very close to her throat. It was temptation to close them about it.

Her fingers pulled at his wrists. "I won't forget again, Zachary. I promise. I—"

He shoved her from him. Her arms flailed to keep her balance as she stumbled backward. The edge of the bed hit her across the back of the legs, and she fell onto it. The rage on his face was terrible, and she cowered before his advance.

"You won't forget it again," he said savagely. "Ross Stone is in town."

She said, "No!" in an almost soundless whisper, and her face blanched.

He sat down on the edge of the bed, watching the terror in her eyes. She was more afraid than he was, and it restored some of his assurance.

"He sent Cleve here ahead of him. I had to kill him. I saw Stone just a few minutes ago. You know why he's here, Valerie?"

She pressed tightly against him, as though she could escape into him and hide. Her face was tight against his chest, and he could hardly make out her words.

"Don't let him find us," she said in a frenzied voice. "Don't let him take Chris. Kill him, Gary."

He let the use of the name slip by. He put a hand under her chin and forced it up. He stared into those fear-distended eyes and said with satisfaction, "You hate him, don't you, Valerie?"

Her eyes closed tightly for a moment, and he wondered what scenes passed behind those lids. She opened her eyes and said, "I hate him." He was satisfied with the vehemence in her voice.

"And he hates both of us," he said. "You know what he'll do if he finds us."

She tried to bury her face again, and he would not let her. "I know," she moaned. "Let's leave, Gary. Let's leave tonight."

"We'll run no more," he said harshly.

Her voice was on the edge of hysteria, but she was not talking to him. She talked to the past. "I never really loved him. All he knew was work. He left me alone on that God-forsaken ranch, and when he was there, he was too tired even to talk. He can't blame me for wanting to live a little."

"But he will," Tanner said relentlessly.

"Kill him, Zachary. Kill him."

If he had any lingering doubts as to her allegiance to the past, it was completely dissipated. "I will," he promised. "He didn't recognize me tonight, but he might recognize you. Don't leave the house until this matter is settled."

She was crying hard, and the tears streaking her cheeks glistened in the lamplight. "I won't. I'd be afraid to."

It was no idle promise. Her fear was very real. He kissed her tear-dampened cheeks, then her lips. They quivered under his mouth, then he felt the response building up in them. At this moment, Ross Stone was very far away.

Chapter Eight

A FAINT gray light came through the room's one window, when Ross awakened in the morning. The man next to him had turned on his side again and was snoring into his ear. He did not know whether the day's first light or the snoring awakened him. He stretched gingerly and got up. He felt more tired than when he had gone to sleep.

After rinsing his face in some water from the crockery bowl near the door, he walked through the saloon and out onto the street. He needed some breakfast and looked for another tent restaurant. This time the food was better. The eggs were only slightly overdone, and the bacon could still be identified as bacon instead of charred strips of something. The matronly woman behind the counter poured him a second cup of coffee, and he smiled his appreciation.

"That's better," she said with satisfaction. "I was wondering if you could."

"I guess it is better," he admitted sheepishly. It came as a shock to realize how his inner thoughts molded his face. He wondered what face he had presented to Lynn Redford, and he thought irritably, Why should it concern you?

He paid the woman and went back to the street. He wanted to find Cleve today, but he had no starting point. It could be a big job, digging him out of this city. He thought about it before he chose his direction. Since Cleve wasn't registered in any of the hotels, boarding houses would be the next most logical bet.

He went from one boarding house to another, asking directions to the next from the last, and at each he received a negative answer. He would name Cleve and describe him, and most of the time interest was gone before he finished. The reaction was always the same—a shake of the head.

By noon, a stubborn worry insisted on creeping in. The boarding houses and hotels were fruitless. Where could Cleve be? He leaned against the pillar of a wooden awning and rolled a cigarette. Had Cleve left because the quarry had taken fright and fled? That could be it; Cleve would stick close. But then Cleve would have left him a letter or eventually send him one, and the Wells Fargo office would be the place to ask for it.

The office was two blocks back, and he reversed his steps. He slowed as he came to a cross street, and a big man lumbered around the corner and almost bumped into him.

The man stepped back, his startled face beefy with swelling.

"Hello, Mack," Ross said sardonically; but he did not miss the savage, almost insane glow in Mack's eyes.

Mack rumbled a string of swear words, but he kept them impersonal. Ross watched him warily. Was Mack prodding himself into further action? He decided he was not, that the incident was over. It was usually that way with a man who had only brute force to rely upon.

He crossed the street, then turned around and looked back. Mack still stood there, an expression of utter malignancy stamping his face. Ross thoughtfully studied the expression before he continued up the street. Perhaps he was a little hasty in deciding it was over. He shrugged and temporarily forgot Mack.

The Wells Fargo office was busy. A freight wagon stood at the platform, and two men were unloading it. They cursed in a steady stream as they unloaded awkward spools of barbed wire. Even leather gloves did not keep them from the wicked nicks of the barbs.

Ross had a rangeman's aversion to wire, but he could recognize the inevitableness of it. As the tide of people pushing west grew stronger, a man would need more of this stuff to protect his land against intrusion. Ross could accept the fact, but it did not make him like it more.

He walked into the office and waited patiently in line until a harassed clerk was free. He gave his name, and the baldheaded little man pulled a stack of letters from a cubbyhole and leafed through them. The process took him considerable time, for he peered nearsightedly through glasses at the writing on each letter.

"Nothing for you, mister," he said, shaking his head to emphasize the words.

Ross knew a start of dismay. He had been so sure that this was the answer. He said, "Are you sure?"

"Damn it," the clerk growled. "Didn't I tell you?" He glared at Ross, but the look faded when he met Ross's eyes.

"You told me," Ross said, keeping his anger in check. "Did he leave word of any kind with you? Was he in here?" He gave the man Cleve's name and started to describe him. Before he was finished the clerk said wearily, "I see hundreds of people every day, most of them newcomers. How do you expect me to remember one?"

The line was piling up behind Ross, and people muttered their impatience. The clerk looked past Ross and said, "Next?"

He stepped aside, and the line moved forward. The worry was greater. It had a lot of space to spread in the growing hollow in his stomach. He walked out of the office and down the street, and for a long moment, the worry took the place of thinking. He knew Cleve had been in Virginia City; the letter from him proved that. But where was he now?

He rolled a cigarette, his eyes narrowed and brooding. He put the worry aside and began to think. He sucked in a long draft of smoke and held it. Had

Cleve run into trouble? Perhaps he'd been forced into hiding until he was sure Ross had arrived.

The tension eased from Ross's face, and he snapped the unfinished cigarette away. That could explain why Cleve had not openly met him. A thread of worry immediately crept into the pattern of his reasoning. How bad was the trouble? The word trouble suggested jail; the law should know of any recent fights.

He found the sheriff's office on a side street. It was a small, dusty room with a cracked green blind at the single window. A battered roll-top desk and two chairs, their sagging strength held together with wire, were the only items of furniture. Wanted posters were on the walls, their writing almost illegible under the fly specks and dust.

A man sitting at the desk looked up at Ross's entrance. His hair was sprinkled with white, and the drooping mustache had long white hairs in it. Age showed in his seamed face and in the gnarled, veined hands, but more of it showed in his manner, in the weariness of the faded blue eyes. Here was a man who had seen much of life, and who was tired of what he had looked at. He wore an ancient vest over a collarless shirt, and a dull star was pinned to the vest.

He spat at the cuspidor beside the desk, and it made a pinging sound under the impact. He said, "Howdy," and waited, his eyes never leaving Ross.

Ross gave his name, and the man said, "Graham." He was sparing with words, as though each took a certain effort.

Ross said, "I'm looking for my brother, Cleve Stone. He's not registered at any of the hotels or boarding houses." He described Cleve, and Graham listened patiently. But he was shaking his head as Ross finished. "If I seen him, I sure don't remember it," he said. He spit again at the cuspidor, and the little pinging sound followed. "That don't mean nothing. With the way people are flocking in here, he could be here six months and I wouldn't know it." His shoulders lifted and fell in a weary gesture that said that the tide of events was now beyond any of his capacities.

His words were a relief, in a way, but it left Ross where he began with no starting point. He said, "I was thinking that if Cleve had been in a fight, you'd know about it."

Graham squinted at him. "I might know if he was killed in a gunfight. They usually call me for that. We get a legal killing almost every day. But an ordinary fight? They break out all over the town every hour. If you're thinking of murder, that could happen. I know men have disappeared. Maybe they wandered off to new diggings without telling nobody, and maybe they didn't." It was a long speech for him, and his face showed it.

The silence grew heavy between them as Ross pulled the words this way and that, trying to lessen their suggestion.

Ross said, "I ran across a man named Tate, in Folsom. Do you know him?"

Graham looked at the tied-down holster, and his

eyes went hard. "You the man who killed him?"

A startled flash appeared in Ross's eyes. Graham might look old and tired, but he kept up with events. He said evenly, "I was forced into it."

The coldness remained in Graham's eyes. "You might've been," he conceded. "Tate was a killer. I ain't saying I'm sorry he's gone. Why'd he jump you?"

"I haven't the slightest idea."

Graham's look was scornful. He said, "You had trouble with Mack. What was that over?"

Ross's eyes held more respect. He shrugged. "Just a disagreement."

Graham snapped, "What's your brother doing here?" His tone said, *If* he is your brother. "And what are you after?"

Ross knew how Graham felt. A lawman was constantly worried about the explosive potentialities of his town. He would have liked to see Graham's face if he said *I came here to kill a man.* He said, "That's personal business, Sheriff."

"Maybe," Graham said pointedly. "When you come in, I thought there was the look of trouble about you. I'm warning you—don't be taking anything into your own hands."

Ross's grin was bleak. "I'm obliged, Sheriff."

He walked down the street, his eyes troubled. Cleve was hiding—or living with somebody else. Ross's mind stubbornly refused to accept any other conjecture. But now where would he look? Covering every tent and shack and house in Virginia City would be a long and tiresome job. His mind jumped ahead. Suppose the trail were lost here—what would he do then? Cut back to the coast and continue north to Oregon? The prospect of the empty days ahead filled him with despondency.

He picked the north end of town, and his questions were rewarded with only negative answers. The tired sun hung on the horizon for a brief moment, flooding the streets with one last fierce blaze of heat, then slowly disappeared. Ross smelled cooking fires, mingled with the appetizing aroma of food. He heard men call to one another, and the loneliness cut like a knife edge.

He was faced with the prospects of another night like the last one, and he could not stand it. Worse was the drain it put upon the meager supply of money he had. A week's stay in this town would just about exhaust it. When it was gone, he would have to go to work here. That had happened before during the search, and the trail always dimmed during lost time. It made him frantic with urgency to think he might be close, then have it slip away. But he could get his bedroll from the livery stable. That would save the cost of sleeping space.

The livery stables! He swore at himself for not having thought of them before. Cleve used some method of transportation to get here. He came either by horse or by stage. And if he had left, he would have to go the same way. If none of the livery stables remembered him, then surely some stage driver would. They might be antagonistic because of what had happened with Mack, but he would meet that when he came to it. He grinned wryly at the thought that Cleve might have ridden with Mack.

He was a block from the livery stable, when a voice hailed him. He turned, and an ancient wagon, pulled by an equally ancient horse, came toward him. Enoch Redford drove the wagon, and he kept waving at Ross as though fearful he would not stop. He pulled to a halt beside Ross and said, "I was hoping I'd run into you. Been keeping an eye open all afternoon."

Ross put a foot up on the wagon and asked, "How's it going, Enoch?" It was good to see this face, eager with friendliness.

"I'm tired," Enoch said. "Moving into a new place is a big job. I did the shopping this afternoon, while Lynn finished cleaning up the house."

Ross looked at the wagon bed. It was filled with assorted sized and shaped packages. A sick man would be little help around a house. Ross suspected Lynn had wanted him out of the way.

Redford said, "Climb in." He chuckled at the inquiry on Ross's face and said, "You're going to eat with us tonight. I had a meal in town this afternoon. I know what kind of food you get here. I can promise you better. Lynn's pretty handy with a pan."

The offer was tempting. There would be companionship for the evening and a good meal. He said, "How will Lynn feel about it?"

"She'll be pleased."

Ross remembered the last expression he had seen on her face. He doubted Redford.

"Climb in," Redford said impatiently. "You want to keep her waiting?"

Ross swung up and sat down beside him. This was probably unwise, but the invitation won him over.

The outskirts of town fell behind them, and Redford said, "My brother staked this claim and built a shack on it. He never had enough money to develop it. He died six months ago and left it to me. Lynn thought we ought to sell it, but I wanted to hang on. I'm glad I did. The Gouge Eye isn't too far from us, and there's a rumor out they've hit a vein. If it runs under our place—" He stopped and stared into the deepening night. "If it does, I can quit worrying about what will happen to Lynn. It's been tough on her the last few years. I ain't been able to work much. I worry about what will happen."

"Sure," Ross said. A woman always seemed to be back of a man's efforts and worries. He thought violently, It won't happen to me again.

Redford said, "The claim must have some value. I've got three letters from a man named Travis, offering to buy it." He scowled out over the back of the horse. "I tried to look him up today in town. Nobody knew of him."

Ross thought about what Redford. said. Travis could have been an assumed name to keep Redford from jacking up the price if he knew the writer's real identity.

Or the man could have gone broke and wandered away.

"Each new offer raised the price," Redford said. "I figured if the property was getting that valuable to Travis, I'd better get up here and see what was happening." He sighed and snapped the reins across the rump of the horse. "Wish I had enough money to sink a real shaft. I guess I'll have to sit here until the land around us proves up, and then maybe sell for the best price I can get."

For an instant, Ross was touched with the pulse-quickening thought of riches, riches torn from the ground. If he had enough money to sink Redford's shaft, a few months' time might make them all rich. He would never be permanently interested in mining, but it could be the springboard to something better. There was good land in this country. With money, he could purchase it and make a new start in the work he wanted; he could build and stock a ranch properly.

Redford said brusquely, "We'll see what happens," as though he were ashamed at revealing so much.

The silence held the remainder of the trip. Ross judged Redford drove a mile from the outskirts of Virginia City. The claim sat in a little clearing, laboriously hacked away by hand. For better than a hundred yards around the cabin the stumps of the trees were mute evidence of the work that had gone into the place. The cabin was a crude affair of small barked logs, chinked with mud against the cold winds of the mountains' winter months. The chimney tilted wearily, and Ross absently watched the smoke trailing from it.

Redford must have guessed at his thoughts, for he said in a discouraged tone, "It ain't much." He pulled up the horse and yelled, "Lynn. I'm home."

She was smiling as she came to the door. She stared at Ross, and the smile was replaced by something very near to dismay. One cheek was smudged, and her hair was in disarray. An apron was pinned up around her waist, and the front of her dress was soiled.

Redford said, "Look who I brought home to supper."

She said indignantly, "Father—" and broke off. She looked at Ross, and color swept into her face. She said sharply, "You can't come in now. The floor's wet. I'll call you." She disappeared, and although the door remained open, Ross had the definite impression of its being slammed shut.

He said uneasily, "Enoch, I'll be moseying along."

"You will not," Redford said. The set of his chin was stubborn as he said, "I invited you, and you'll stay. This ain't like Lynn at all," he muttered.

They smoked in uneasy silence for the better part of ten minutes. Lynn reappeared in the doorway and called, "Come in." Her voice was no more cordial.

Ross stepped inside the cabin. The plank flooring had been thoroughly scrubbed, but it had been some time ago, for no trace of dampness remained. He looked at her and saw how she had used the time. She wore a clean dress, and her face was washed. Her hair was in order, and she looked fresh and young.

She colored under his quizzical inspection, and for

an instant he thought she was going to be angry. She managed a laugh, and it was almost gay. "No woman likes to be caught by anyone looking the way I looked then, Mr. Stone."

He smiled at her and she returned it, and for a moment he felt something warm and vital between them. It was gone as quickly as it appeared, and again the invisible wall was up.

She said without looking at him, "Supper will be ready in twenty minutes."

He caught the unwillingness of her tone and said with a degree of heat, "Look, I didn't want to come. Enoch insisted."

She gave him a quick flash of her eyes. "You're welcome," she said. He was certain she intended saying something else, but she turned away.

He asked, "Is there anything I can do?"

She said over her shoulder, "You can get me some wood."

He worked out his irritation on a small log, cutting and splitting a double armload. A ghost of a smile was in her eyes as he dumped the last load beside the stove. He had the feeling she knew every thought running through his mind.

He sat down to a good. meal. The meat was done to a turn, and the fried potatoes were not soggy. Some time during the day shc had baked. It had been a long time since he had eaten bread of that lightness and texture. He spoke his appreciation and saw the pleasure on her face.

Redford said, "I'll clear the table."

His aim was apparent—he wanted to give them time alone—and Ross saw the anger flash in her eyes.

"I'll help you," he said stubbornly. He wanted no time alone with her.

She stood up and said, "I want to talk to you, Mr. Stone."

He walked outside with her, and the evening breeze carried the scent of the mountain down to them. There was a soft yellow light in the sky, though the moon was not yet in sight.

She said, "I want to give you this."

He turned his head and saw the money in her hand.

She said, "It was thoughtful of you, but we didn't need it." He didn't respond, and she said, "You must believe we are grateful."

He turned and said bluntly, "But you don't like me."

Her eyes met his readily enough, but there was that mental retreating within her. "I've seen only one side of you, Mr. Stone. In Folsom we heard that you had killed a man. I saw you manhandle the baggage master. I saw your fight with the stage driver."

He stared at her in outrage. In none of those cases could he have acted differently. He amended that a little. Perhaps he could have with the baggage master.

Her smile had an odd, wistful quality. "I know now why you fought with the driver. You didn't have to. Not because of me."

"Do you always believe in turning the other cheek, Miss Redford?" She had judged and condemned him, and he wouldn't give her a chance to speak. So she had seen only one side of him. Well, that was the side he wanted to stick in her mind.

He said harshly, "Do you know why I came to Virginia City? I came here to kill a man—and a woman—if I can find them."

He threw the words at her brutally, and he heard her quickened breathing. She said a small, "Oh," and her face looked strained. She put a long, searching look on him, then turned. She walked rapidly back to the cabin.

He started off, not wanting to talk to either of them. He could say his apology to Redford later.

"Ross, hold up," he heard Redford call.

He turned reluctantly, and Redford came up, panting a little from his hurried walk. He said, "Ross, don't judge her too hard."

"It looks as if she does all the judging."

Redford said in a soft voice, "She's afraid of violence, Ross. She was going to be married. Her man killed another. It wasn't a fair fight, because he had to run. Something like that leaves its mark, and it takes a time to get over it."

Ross looked at the cabin. He understood her better now and, he thought violently, he did not want that understanding of her. He wanted nothing forming between them.

He said gruffly, "I understand, Enoch. Tell her I enjoyed the supper. Don't hitch up. I want to walk in."

"Ross," Redford said, then stopped. His face was troubled. He said lamely, "Come out again, whenever you feel like it."

Chapter Nine

H E WALKED the distance back to town slowly. He kept seeing Lynn in the various moods she had shown him. He didn't know her well, and wished she would not loom so large in his mind. But he couldn't forget her troubles.

He passed the first shanty on the outskirts of town. It was still fairly early, but most of the houses were dark. The two squares that formed the business district were ablaze with lights, and he heard the blast of noise coming from them. The night's revelry was well under way. For an instant he considered a drink or a series of them, then he pushed the thought away. No, it was best to go directly to the livery stable, pick up his bedroll, and try to keep a clear head for tomorrow. Damn Redford for inviting him to dinner.

He passed two shanties standing side by side, and half a block ahead of him the houses were solidly lined. Some instinct touched him and he stopped, staring into the darkness ahead. He had the feeling that his every movement was being watched, and he stood for a long moment before he moved on with slow, careful steps, feeling the tightness that stretched his skin. The hunted and the hunter both knew that tightness, the one from being stalked, the other from the act of stalking. He was not sure which he was.

He passed the first house at the head of the block. There was a bush of some kind at the corner of the yard, and as he approached it, a bulking shadow stepped out from it. The shadow stopped squarely across the walk, and in the darkness Ross could not recognize the man. He slowed his pace until he was barely moving, and every sense was alert. This might or might not be a chance encounter, and he was preparing for any direction it could take. He was within three feet of the man before he identified him. Some of the tightness left him. He had been up against this situation before. He said, "Yes?" in a flat voice and waited. It was Mack's move.

Mack's voice contained a note of triumph. "I've been waiting for you." He made no forward move, and that was odd.

If Mack intended renewing the fight, he was slow about it, yet he could be here for no other reason. It put an uncertainty in Ross, and the tightness came back.

He said in that same flat voice, "Step out of the way, Mack," and started forward.

A slight scuffling sound behind him warned him. He tried to turn in time but the movement was awkward and inept. No wonder Mack had seemed so sure; there was help for him behind that bush. He threw up an arm, and the descending club, instead of hitting him squarely on the head, wasted part of its power against his protective arm. It slid along his arm and glanced off the side of his head, putting a numbing chain around most of his senses. He tried to drive forward against his attacker, and his knees insisted upon buckling. Blackness, deeper than the night, hovered all around him, reaching for him with snaky little tendrils.

A hand seized his shoulder and spun him around. Mack's fist smashed into his face, breaking his lips. Instead of further dulling him, the sharp sting of his broken flesh drove some of the blackness away. There were at least two of them, and with the way things were going the odds were bad.

Mack had set this up, and Ross's rage exploded inside him, acting as a stimulus against the hurt. He said savagely, "God damn you, Mack," and lurched forward a step, his hands groping for any kind of a hold. They might smash him down, but not before he could punish Mack.

His hands caught Mack's arms and pulled him close. He hung on with desperate intensity, buying time for his head to clear. He buried his face in Mack's shirt front, and the roughness of the fabric scratched his cheek. Mack struggled to throw him off, and blows rained upon Ross from behind. He turned Mack, using him as a shield against those blows, and heard Mack yell in a frenzied voice, "Get him! Damn it, get him!"

Ross's vision was better, and the weakness was losing some of its grip. He saw now that there had been not one but two men behind the bush. So the odds were too high, but one thought burned fiercely in his mind. He was going to hurt Mack as much as he could.

He swung Mack around, blocking a rush by one of the others to get at him, and Mack's cursing had a note of wildness in it. The thought struck Ross with force. If he could break Mack in a hurry, it might lessen the others' determination.

He jerked his knee in a vicious upward thrust, ramming it into Mack's groin. Mack's breath puffed out in an explosive gasp, half whistle and half groan. Ross felt the limpness run through Mack, and he let go of him with one hand. He chopped the hand viciously into Mack's face. He hit him again and again, and the sagging was pronounced when he let go of him completely.

Mack fell, and Ross tried to step over the bulky body. Mack had enough strength left to throw out his arms, and the hands pulled at Ross's feet. The effort was not powerful enough to send him down, but he had to flail his arms wide to keep his balance.

It left him unprotected, and the end of the club poked into his face. He felt it grinding against his nose, and the pain was like an explosion bursting before his face. One of them kicked him in the stomach, and it turned his muscles into quivering string. His body wanted to go down, but a tiny spark still flamed inside him, keeping him on his feet. He forced his legs wide, trying to brace himself against the weaving that threatened to upset him. His hands groped blindly before him, wanting a hold on anything that would support him.

Mack was crawling away from him, and Ross kicked at him, trying to pin him down. The kick thudded home, but there was no force to it. He tried to follow Mack, and a fist smashed into his face, driving him back. The blows seemed to come at him from every side, and his heavy, awkward arms could not block them. He was vaguely aware that Mack was getting to his feet, and he could not stop him from doing it. Mack's voice was almost a scream, and its shrillness penetrated the fog growing in Ross's mind.

"I'll kill you for this," Mack yelled. "I'll kill you for this."

They swarmed at him, their combined weight carrying him to the ground. His blows were weak and ineffectual, not even checking any of them. He felt the jolt as he hit the ground, but unconsciousness was not far away. The kicking kept up even after all signs of life were gone from him. The inert body jolted this way and that, following the force of the kick. Mack drove one final kick into the body at his feet and said with ugly satisfaction, "That'll teach the bastard." His words were jerky against the panting of his voice.

All three of them breathed hard, now that the physical force of their violence was spent. The enraged twist of their features straightened, and they looked uneasily at each other.

One of them knelt beside Ross, bent low, and listened for a moment. He raised his head and said, "I think he's dead, Mack."

"Good," Mack said savagely. He was five hundred dollars richer, and the blot on his reputation was removed. He turned his head toward the beginning of the street, then said, "Somebody coming. We'd better leave."

They went down the street, the three furtive shadows.

There was no conversation among them at all.

The moon came up full, its soft light bathing the broken, battered figure in the dusty street.

Chapter Ten

REDFORD drove his wagon into the head of the street and peered ahead. "Guess I missed him," he muttered. He had thought he would catch up with Ross before now. He decided to turn back because he knew it would be impossible to spot Ross among all the people in the heart of town.

He was pulling on the rein to turn the horse when he saw a dark blotch of shadow lying in the street near the walk. There was something unnatural about that, and he stood up in the box in an effort to better see. "Hell," he said with a sudden, sharp catch of breath. That was a man lying there, and there was a limp sprawl about him that could only mean one of two things—he was either dead or extremely drunk. Redford gave the first the most consideration. This man was too far from the saloons for a drunk to wander.

He halted the horse beside the inert form and stared down at it. "Ross," he said, with a queer break in his voice. He leaped to the ground and knelt down beside him. He picked up one of the hands, and it seemed lifeless to his touch. "Damn!" he said, and there was bitter protest to the word.

He pulled out a handkerchief and dabbed at the bloody face. It was a futile, helpless gesture, for no one could do anything for a dead man. The cut on the right cheekbone oozed blood, and Redford stared at it, his mind groping for an isolated fact. His breathing was a gusty sound as he found the fact. Dead men did not bleed.

He bent his head close and heard the faint sighing of Ross's breath. Ross was horribly battered, but at the moment he lived.

Redford glanced fearfully around. He did not know how this had been done, or how many had done it, but he would bet it was more than one. They might be watching him now; they might come back.

He found strength in his agony of fear and concern for Ross. He tugged at his shoulders and dragged him to the tail-gate of the wagon. He heard the groan that escaped Ross's lips. He lowered the tail-gate and lifted the upper part of Ross's body enough to get his shoulder under it. The dead, limp weight took tremendous effort to lift. He got the upper half of Ross's body into the wagon, then lifted the legs and tumbled him inside.

The sense of urgency still drove him, and his hands trembled as he fastened the tail-gate. He had to stop for a moment and lean against it to catch his breath. He felt a hollow fire inside him, and his legs were shaky. He hauled himself up onto the seat and lashed at the horse. He felt naked and afraid. The men who had done that to Ross would not hesitate to do the same for anyone trying to help him. He wanted to get out of here, he wanted to get the security of his own walls around him.

He kept the horse at the peak of its capacity, forgetting the battering this gait gave the unconscious man in back. He was almost to his cabin before sanity touched him. He stopped the wagon and looked behind him. Ross was lying face up. A hand moved feebly, as though he wanted to touch his face.

He moved the horse on at a slower pace, and he was calling when he came in sight of the cabin. "Lynn!" he shouted. "Lynn. Come out here."

He saw her silhouetted in the doorway, then she was running toward the wagon. "What is it?" she gasped. "What's happened?"

He did not stop the wagon until he reached the door. Lynn ran along side of it. "It's Ross," he said. "He's badly beaten."

He heard the sharp break in her breathing as she looked at Ross; then her breathing steadied, and she said in a level voice, "We've got to get him inside and into bed."

"We sure do," he agreed fervently.

Their combined strength was barely equal to the task of getting Ross out of the wagon and into the house. They dragged him more than they carried him, and both were panting for breath when they laid him across the bed.

Lynn stared at him, and a shudder ran through her. A splotch of blood was smeared across the bodice of her dress.

"Undress him." Her voice was calm enough. "I'll heat some water."

Redford tugged off the boots, then the pants. He tore Ross's shirt in taking it off.

Ross had taken a fearful beating. His face was bloody from half a dozen cuts, and it was beginning to swell. By morning it would be beyond recognition. The upper part of his body was a mass of discoloration, and the flesh was puffy under Redford's gentle fingers. It felt as though there was a broken rib or two on Ross's badly bruised right side.

Lynn came back with a pan of hot water and all the towels she had. She gently bathed Ross's face. It took her the better part of an hour and several pans of water before Ross was cleansed and bandaged. She wrapped several strips of bandage around his sides, and her hands remained steady and efficient until the job was finished. Then the shaking started in them. Her anxiety showed in her eyes as she looked at her father.

"Sure, he'll live," Redford said. His face looked gray and drawn in the lamplight. "He's as strong as an ox."

Lynn covered her face with her hands, and her shoulders shook. Her voice was barely audible as she said, "Why do men do this to each other?"

Redford petted her shoulder with a clumsy hand. His voice had a helpless note. "I don't know, honey. I don't know."

Tanner could not settle himself. Earlier in the evening Mack had promised him some news, and he couldn't sit calmly and wait for it. He opened a drawer and pulled out a squat, brown bottle. He uncapped it, tilted it to his lips, and gulped several times, feeling better as the authority of the liquor spread throughout his stomach.

He stiffened as he heard the heavy tread in the hall outside the door. He knew that walk; it was Mack's. But there was a difference about it tonight. It sounded heavier than usual as though it were hard for Mack to move. He placed his hands on the desk and forced them into a relaxed position. His face was composed and cold as the door opened.

There was a noticeable limp in Mack's walk as he crossed the room to the desk. His face showed a fresh cut, and a bruise was blossoming on his right cheek. Tanner knew a sinking dismay as he watched him. Had Mack failed again? He held back his anxious questions and waited for Mack to speak.

Mack put his knuckles on the desk's edge. "Give me my five hundred," he said.

Elation swelled inside Tanner. He kept it from showing on his face. "It looks as if he did a little beating in his own right, Mack."

Mack's words were a string of dripping obscenity. Tanner waited for him to run down. He listened to raw, animal hatred with no subtlety to it. Mack took a breath and said, "He'll never beat anyone else. I kicked the life out of him."

Now it took an effort to keep the elation from showing. Tanner wanted details, but he must not let Mack know he was too curious. However, he might be able to anger Mack into telling him a little of what had happened.

"How many did it take, Mack?"

Mack's face turned raw and violent. His fists clenched, and he shouted, "I did it by myself."

His reaction was too violent, his defense too belligerent. Mack had the help of at least another, perhaps more. It gave Tanner a greater confidence in Mack's assertion. Stone was a powerful man, and Mack had not been able to handle him before by himself. It might take two or more to get Stone off his feet, but once down, Tanner knew Mack would kick him to death.

"Sure, Mack," he said soothingly. He opened a desk drawer and pulled out a packet of bills. He saw the greed shining in Mack's eyes as he counted off a thin sheaf of them. He. pushed the bills toward Mack and laughed. "I should have known better than to bet against you."

He stood up, walked around the desk and placed a hand on Mack's shoulder. His voice was filled with admiration as he said, "I don't think there's a man in the world who can stand up against you." He turned Mack and walked him toward the door. Tanner closed the door behind him and beat his hands together in an excess of joy. He could walk the streets of this town and never know a worry.

His mind turned to the business he had neglected since Stone's arrival. So the Redfords had refused his offers by letter and were now here. But old Redford would never develop that claim. He would be glad to leave it after a visit Tanner had in mind. He opened the door to call Jude and Rezin, then remembered he had sent them to Folsom yesterday on another matter. They wouldn't be returning for a day or two. Tanner nodded in slow deliberation. That was what fear did to a man—it made him forget details, and details were always important. Let the Redfords stay another day or so. It would not be hard for Jude and Rezin to run them off at any time.

Ross stirred, and regretted the movement. It sent waves of pain washing throughout his body. He opened his eyes and stared in bewilderment about him. He was lying in a bed, and he had no recollection of getting here. Someone must have helped him. He lifted a hand and felt the bandages on his head. Whoever that someone was, they had taken good care of him.

He heard movement beyond the curtain that cut off the bed and said a tentative, "Hello."

The curtains parted, and Lynn Redford stepped to the side of the bed. Her face looked tired and drawn, and the dark shadows under her eyes were evidence that she had missed a good deal of sleep.

"Who brought me here last night?" he asked.

"Not last night," she said. "Two nights ago."

"I've been out that long?" he said incredulously.

Her nod was a tired gesture. "We've been worried about you. I sent Father after you to apologize for my discourtesy—particularly after we owed you so much. He found you lying in the street."

He stared at her and felt the tight, icy wall he had built around his heart beginning to melt.

He smiled and said, "I think the account is more than squared. I'm grateful, Lynn."

She did not respond to the smile. "Mack did it, didn't he?"

His face turned hard and cruel. "Yes."

Her voice was low. "It started with his violence to us. You punished him for it, and he beat you for that punishment. Now, you will look for him again."

"I'll find him," he said flatly.

"Don't you see it's an endless chain?" she cried. "Even if you kill him, he has friends. His friends will pick it up, and it will go on and on."

He saw that there could never be a permanent bond between them. She disapproved of too many things about him. His burden, since he came to Virginia City, was tripled. He had to find Cleve. He had to find Gary Anson. Now Mack was added to the list. He knew a savage desire to alienate her—and himself from her. "I told you why I came here. Only now I'm going to kill two men."

She reached out a hand, but stopped it before it touched his arm. "You talked about the first one while you were unconscious."

The savage desire was still with him. "Did I talk about my wife, who ran away with him? I could have let her go and never taken a step after her. But she took my son with them. Chris was three, and he belonged with me, not with her." He stared at the far wall, his face cold and immobile. He was not talking to her but to the destiny that controlled him. "I'm not even sure he's alive."

"Ross—" she whispered.

He turned his head from her. He needed nothing from her and wanted nothing. "I'll leave today."

"You can't," she said in quick protest. "You're in no condition—"

"I'm leaving," he interrupted harshly.

Their stubborn wills met head-on and clashed. "All right," she snapped. "I'll get your clothes."

The curtains waved angrily after her violent departure through them. She had a temper, he reflected. And he had the knack of too readily striking sparks from it. He wouldn't let it happen again.

She came back with his clothes and laid them on the edge of the bed. She placed his boots on the floor beneath them. The shirt was clean and mended. She did not look at him as she said, "If you want anything, I'll be outside."

He ignored the tentative overture. He would not have any more of her touches softening him.

He heard the outer door slam behind her and smiled bleakly at the volume of the sound. She disliked him as much as he disliked her.

He found out how weak he was when he dressed. The pain had subsided into a dull throbbing, but his muscles seemed to fight his commands. He was breathing hard when he finished stuffing his shirt into his pants. He buttoned the pants and sat down on the edge of the bed. A few moments ago, he had been comfortable there, with none of this throbbing pain, and certainly with none of this weakness. He made a grimace. He should have listened more and talked less.

It took effort to tug on his boots. As worn as they were, they had a hell of a lot of resistance. He stood up and grabbed the foot of the bed for support. He took a deep breath and moved toward the curtains. The first few steps were wobbly, but he could make it. He stopped in the center of the cabin and looked about him, knowing an odd reluctance to leave. A pot of soup was just beginning to bubble on the stove, and its savory aroma filled the room. His belly rumbled disconsolately; he should have waited until after the noon meal before he offended her.

His hat, gunbelt and gun were hanging on a peg near the door, and he moved toward them. That walk into town seemed a huge task. He guessed he was going to have to ask Enoch for a lift.

He turned his head toward the door. He thought he heard angry words coming from outside, and he stiffened as he heard a woman scream. That could be only Lynn. He jerked the pistol from its holster and sprang toward the door. The damned door fought him, and his cursing was broken because his breathing was ragged. He finally flung open the door and froze at what he saw.

Sixty feet in front of the cabin Enoch Redford was on the ground, one hand pressed against his forehead, the other plucking in uncertain motions at the dirt. A red line leaked from between the fingers of the hand against his head. A man stood over him, grinning crookedly. He still held a raised gun in his hand, and he looked as though he were ready to strike Redford again with the barrel.

Lynn struggled in the grip of another man. Her screaming had stopped, and there was only rage on her face. Her blouse was torn, and Ross saw the whiteness of a shoulder. He remembered how fine the texture of her skin was.

He drew deep on his lungs and bellowed, "Hold it." The blast of sound jerked all heads toward him. The tableau held for a moment; then the man standing over Redford broke it by swinging his gun toward Ross. Ross shot him in the chest and heard the deep grunt of shock before the man went down. He fell across Redford's legs, and there was an instant inertness about him that told he was dead. Ross could not shoot at the other one for fear of hitting Lynn.

He shouted and plunged forward. The man released Lynn and ran. He kept her between Ross and his direction of flight. Ross stepped to one side, then the other, trying to get a clear shot at him. Each time the man would dart back into line, and Ross was afraid to risk a shot. If Lynn would only drop to the ground, but she stood there as though incapable of movement.

Ross did not get his shot until he had reached her, and by then the man was a hundred feet away and moving fast. Ross steadied his breathing against his rage and exertion. He pulled down on the fleeing figure and fired. He thought he saw him stagger, but he was not certain. The man disappeared into a fringe of brush and was out of sight.

Ross started to follow him, and Lynn seized his arm. "Help him," she sobbed. Her voice was near hysteria.

Ross stopped, breathing hard. The burst of exertion had wiped out the weakness, but now it came back stronger than ever. He mentally cursed his shaking legs. He wanted to follow the man; he wanted one more shot at him. The crashing noise of the man's flight was growing fainter. With the start he had and the cover of the timber, Ross doubted he could come in sight of him again.

He turned his head and asked in a panting voice, "Lynn. Are you all right?"

She was; the only thing wrong with her was fear that her father had been seriously hurt.

He checked her motion toward Redford. "I'll look," he said quietly.

He walked to Redford and rolled the body off his legs. Redford sat up, and comprehension filled his eyes. Ross leaned over and examined his wound. The gun barrel had split the skin along the forehead for a distance of three inches, but it looked worse than it actually was. Ross looked at Lynn and said, "He's all right."

She came flying toward them and helped Ross get Redford on his feet. With both of them supporting him, Redford took a shaky step. He looked at his bloodied hand, then at the body, lying on the ground. Rage was beginning to fill his voice. "Why, damn them!" he said.

"Who were they?" Ross snapped.

Redford shook his head. "I never saw either of them before." He looked at Lynn, the worry crinkles squeezing his eyes. "You all right, honey?"

She nodded several times as though she were trying to convince herself as much as him.

"What was it all about?" Ross asked.

Redford shook his head. "Damned if I know. I saw them talking to Lynn. When I came up, that one hit me."

Lynn shook her head at the question in Ross's eyes. "I don't know, Ross. One of them grabbed me. The other one hit Father. I guess you heard me scream then."

"Were they drunk?"

Both Redford and Lynn gave the question some thought, and both answered no. "I think I would have smelled it," Lynn said. "As close as he held me." She looked at the dead man, and Ross expected to see her shudder. The angry look remained in her eyes.

"Ross," she said, a wondering quality in her voice. "After I saw him hit Father, I was glad when you shot him. Even now, I can't say I'm sorry he's dead."

He scowled at the dead man, a series of unanswered questions running through his mind. Were these men ordinary claim-jumpers? If so, they had gone about it in an odd way. Had they wandered by, seen Lynn, and been tempted by her fresh loveliness? He could have entertained that question more if they had been drunk. But a sober man did not touch a strange woman unless he wanted the entire country after him. Besides, there were too many free and easy women in Virginia City for a man to be too tempted. He wished he knew what was back of this; he wished he knew if those two were on their own, or if someone had sent them.

He said, "Lynn, go on to the house."

A flash of rebellion appeared in her eyes, but then she meekly turned and obeyed. He thought with wry humor, that her action surprised both of them equally.

He said, "Enoch, I wish I had dropped the other one."

"You think he'll be back."

"I think there's a damned good chance," Ross said slowly. If the man returned, he would not be alone.

His frown deepened as he surveyed the cabin and its site. There were two blank walls in the cabin, and it sat too close to the timber. Sneaking crawlers could get much too near before they could be seen.

He said, "Give me a hand with him." He stopped and picked up the body under its arms.

Redford grunted as he lifted the feet. They carried the body several hundred yards from the cabin and left it in a small clearing. Maybe the man's friends would return for him, and maybe they would not.

They walked back toward the cabin, and Redford said savagely, "This is all I've got. They ain't going to take it away from me." He looked at Ross, and a scared look was in his eyes. "Ross, you're going to stay around for a while, ain't you?"

Ross thought of the man's handling of Lynn. "I'm going to stay." He scowled at the cabin. It was going to be hell to protect. If there were only some way of knowing potential attackers were near before they were close enough to smother the cabin's defenders. His face brightened. There might be a way.

"Enoch," he said. "Hitch up the horse. The Wells Fargo office has some barbed wire. Pick up as many spools as they'll let you have."

Chapter Eleven

TANNER was in an expansive mood. The one source of his fear was removed, and he was on his way to acquiring greater riches. There was no doubt that the Gouge Eye vein extended under Redford's property, and about now, the old man was probably packing. Tanner grinned crookedly. After his fright, Redford would be tickled to take any kind of an offer.

He heard footsteps coming down the hall and took his feet off the desk. That should be Jude and Rezin coming back to tell him they were successful. He would have to contact Redford before the old man left and buy his claim. The closer a man stayed to legalities the less future trouble he had.

The door opened, and Rezin came in. The left shoulder of his shirt was bloody, and his face was pinched with pain. His weight came down hard on his heels as he crossed the office floor, the walk of a hurt man.

A dozen conjectures flashed through Tanner's mind. Had the old man put up a fight? But he had sent two of them against Redford, and they should have been able to handle him. Had the girl taken a hand—or a gun? It did not seem possible, an old man and a girl running off Rezin and Jude.

He snapped, "Where's Jude? What happened?"

Rezin sat down in a chair and stared at Tanner. The look in his eyes was a mixture of pain, and hatred directed at Tanner. He lifted his blood-smeared right hand and touched his shoulder. A wince crossed his face at the gesture.

"Jude's dead," he said dully. He continued to stare at Tanner.

Tanner swore at him. "What happened?" he demanded again.

Rezin took a long time before he answered. He said, "We did it just like you told us. I grabbed the girl, and the old man came up." He put long pauses between each sentence, pauses that tore at Tanner. "Jude knocked the old man down and told him we was coming back for the girl tonight."

Bewilderment spread on Tanner's face. Everything had gone according to schedule. But Jude was dead and Rezin was wounded.

Rezin's eyes grew hot. "You said there were only the two of them out there?"

"Who else was there?" Tanner asked hoarsely. An old fear always left a fertile ground and seeds ready to sprout.

"A big guy," Rezin said. "I never saw him before. He came to the door and killed Jude with one shot.

A long shot. I saw some bandages on him before I run. I kept the girl between me and him and got away. He knocked the corner off my shoulder before I hit the woods. He can shoot." He said the last with a deliberate emphasis, and his eyes never left Tanner's face.

Tanner's hand eased open the desk drawer and closed about the butt of a gun. That growing wildness in Rezin's eyes could mean anything, and it was well to be ready for it.

Rezin's tone was almost reflective. "Jude and I been together a long time. You said nobody else would be there, God damn you!" He grabbed for his gun.

"Don't," Tanner snapped, and the gun in his hand emphasized his command. The fear was back with him again, tearing at his guts. A big man with a bruised and battered face. It could be only Stone, but how had he gotten up after Mack left him, and how was he tied in with the Redfords?

Rezin's hand fell away from his gun, but the hate remained in his eyes.

Tanner leaned forward, and his face was earnest. "I didn't know he was there, Rezin. I'll give you another crack at him tonight. You'll have enough help so there will be no doubt."

Some of the heat left Rezin's eyes. "I want another crack at him," he said almost dreamily. "For Jude." He stared long at Tanner and said, "Maybe you didn't know he was there."

His tone carried a poorly hidden threat. It said, Set it

up right, Tanner, or I'll hold you responsible for Jude. He got to his feet and said, "I'll be back."

Tanner laid the gun on the desk. The urgency of the moment was over. But it would return if anything else went wrong. Rezin had to blame someone for Jude's death.

He said, "Find Mack and send him here."

Rezin nodded and closed the door behind him.

He was standing by the door, gun in hand, when he heard the heavy footsteps coming down the hall. Mack opened the door and stepped into the office. "Rezin said you wanted—" His words broke off as he stared at the empty desk. His head was beginning to turn to search the room, when Tanner hit him with his left hand with all the power he had, catching Mack on the cheekbone. The blow did little more than rock Mack's head back.

Mack was astounded. He fell back a step and said, "What the hell?" His eyes widened at the sight of the gun Tanner held.

"I ought to kill you," Tanner raged. "You damned liar!"

He advanced a step, and the gun muzzle stabbed into Mack's belly.

The madness in Tanner's eyes touched Mack with icy fingers. He backed before the gun and wet his lips, his hands flinging out in unconscious appeal. His stiff tongue had trouble forming the dry, brittle words. "I don't know what you're talking about," he mumbled.

Tanner tried to control his rage. "You lied about killing him, didn't you, Mack?" he said.

The confusion on Mack's face was real as he struggled to understand what was happening. He moved his lips several times before he said, "Who you talking about?"

"You collected five hundred from me, didn't you?"

Mack said incredulously, "You mean him? I did kill him. I kicked the life out of him and left him lying in the street. Hell," he exploded. "He couldn't be alive."

Tanner resisted the impulse to slash the gun barrel across that stupid, brutish face. "But he is. He's out at the Redfords'. What connection does he have with them?"

"An old man and a girl?" Mack asked. His face was sullen. He did not want to tell Tanner this, but he was afraid not to. "It started with them. He claimed I forced them off the road."

The murderous rage surged through Tanner again. So that was the cause of the first fight. Mack had brought the Redfords and Ross Stone together. That, alone, was reason enough to kill him.

The thoughts were written plainly on Tanner's face.

Mack yelled, "Wait, boss. I'll settle him. This time, I'll bring you his damned head."

Tanner studied him with cold eyes. "You will, or you'll lose yours. Make your plans with Rezin. Take as many men as you need."

Some of Mack's aplomb was returning. "What about the Redfords?"

"You want them walking around saying you killed him?"

"No, by hell!" Mack roared.

"Then you know what to do."

Mack walked to the door and looked back at him. The fear was fading from his eyes, and the speculative interest in them would strengthen. Tanner could read the thoughts behind them. Why was he so intent on seeing the big man killed? He regretted that Mack's curiosity was aroused, but it couldn't be helped now.

The swagger was back in Mack's walk as he stepped through the doorway. His words floated back to Tanner. "I'll see you later."

Tanner walked to the window and stared out. Four horsemen rode down the street. They passed from one yellow strip to another, and Tanner's eyes burned. Even without the light he could have recognized Mack's huge bulk and Rezin's slim wiriness. Four men. His face was troubled. He would have liked to see more. He swore and shook his head. The girl didn't count, and the old man was little more. The odds were bad for Ross Stone. Tanner's smile was tight. He could trust the hating of Rezin and Mack to make the attack a quick surprise.

Darkness was almost complete when Ross finished unlooping the last coil of wire from the final spool. Barbed wire was wicked stuff to handle. Leather gloves protected his hands, but his shirt sleeves above them were torn, and his forearms were covered with little stinging cuts. The wire lay in snaky loops around a perimeter two hundred yards from the cabin. It had taken a great deal of effort to lay in through the timber and brush. Lying in loose folds this way, it was deadly stuff. Tight wire would cut man and beast, but it would also throw them back. This stuff would leap off the ground and hopelessly entangle either man or horse. The more they fought it, the more entangled they would become.

Redford said, "I'd hate to be coming up against this."

Ross nodded and looked at the sky. The night was cloudy, and he prayed it would remain that way. He wanted no moonlight reflecting on wire to give it away.

He hoped he was borrowing trouble, that nothing would happen tonight. But a dead man out there and his partner who escaped said differently.

Redford was excited. It showed in the jerkiness of his words. "What do we do now, Ross?"

"Wait," Ross said. The waiting would wear them down, and his worry would increase in proportion to the waiting. The responsibility of the old man and the girl was a big one. He hoped he was right in trying to defend them in this isolated cabin, rather than taking them into town, where they were surrounded by people. But he remembered Graham's suspicious attitude and doubted the sheriff would even listen to him; let alone extend them his protection.

He walked toward the cabin, and Redford followed him. Lynn waited inside, her face white and drawn. Her eyes questioned him, and he tried to put reassurance in his nod. He said, "Leave the lamp on, Lynn."

A light in the cabin would be a normal thing; it would also be a beacon beckoning on any possible marauders. She held a small pistol in her hand, and he added, "Keep it handy, Lynn."

Her actions and expression were those of a sleep-walker, and he said impatiently, "Lynn."

She said in a small voice, "I heard you."

"When we leave, Lynn," he said. "I want you to lie down there." He pointed to the far corner. "And stay there until I come for you." She stared at him, and he asked roughly, "Do you understand me?"

She nodded, and he said to Redford, "Let's go, Enoch."

Outside, Redford nervously fingered his rifle. Ross said, "Keep your head, Enoch. If they come, let them hit the wire before you shoot."

"Ross," Redford said abruptly. "I'm scared."

Ross touched his shoulder. "Sure," he said. "Me, too." He was—not for himself, but for a girl and an old man.

He stationed Redford in front of the cabin, putting him in the deep shadow of a bush. He wanted the back of the cabin for himself, thinking that any attempt would probably be a sneaking one.

He lay down. If more than one man came, they could hit the cabin from any side.

Once the clouds rifted, and the moon shone through. Ross cursed its soft light on the looped coils of wire. Now the barbs had a double edge, biting back against

prise and shock
and given to the

nd the night was
he insects were
to be holding its
ment, and some
ran icily along

ide with infinite
blackness of the
as he heard the
a relief that the
sound again, but
ed. The soft duff
b each hoof-fall.
or the creak of
g. He would not
, until the action

ith a violence so
d of silence was
t and a muttered
nd the sound was
e noise was dou-
horse, and their
threshing grew in
ened. Those loose
fs and legs of the
ngled them more.

He knew a quick regret

the high, frightened ye

sound came from the fr

"Enoch," he yelled in

feet. A horse reared, and

rider in his rifle sights.

the butt pounded back a

scream broke off on its

figure slide limply from

again.

He ran forward a few

one. The rider squalled

rise and fall as he tried to

took a bucking jump, and

Ross heard the ripping o

the animal's plunge to

instant before the horse

the rider from his seat.

and kicking in the wire.

plunging first one way,

each convulsive lunge u

Ross heard a shot fro

turned and ran that way.

himself as he ran. He did

firing at the sound of new

ford, and the old man wa

"Two of them, Ross. I

the saddle. The other's ho

get a shot at him. He's ca

Ross listened to the m

Ross and Enoch. The benefit of surprise and shock would be lost to Ross and Redford and given to the others.

The clouds drifted together again, and the night was dark and still. For a moment even the insects were quiet, and every living thing seemed to be holding its breath. Ross went tight during that moment, and some deep instinct came to the surface and ran icily along his skin. Something was out there.

He turned his head from side to side with infinite care, his eyes trying to penetrate the blackness of the night. He let out a soft, long breath as he heard the thud of hoof against rock. It was a relief that the waiting was over. He did not hear the sound again, but that did not mean the horse had stopped. The soft duff of the forest would cushion and absorb each hoof-fall.

He listened for another hoof sound or the creak of saddle leather, and there was nothing. He would not even know how many were out there, until the action broke.

As prepared as he was, it broke with a violence so sudden that it startled him. The void of silence was broken by a horse's frightened snort and a muttered curse. The horse bugled its terror, and the sound was followed by a threshing of hoofs. The noise was doubled by the movements of another horse, and their rearing up spotted them for him. The threshing grew in volume, and he knew what had happened. Those loose wire coils had wrapped about the hoofs and legs of the horses, and their struggles only entangled them more.

He knew a quick regret for the horses. Then he heard the high, frightened yells of the riders, and a similar sound came from the front of the cabin.

"Enoch," he yelled in warning and jumped to his feet. A horse reared, and he caught the dark mass of its rider in his rifle sights. He squeezed the trigger, and the butt pounded back against his shoulder. The man's scream broke off on its highest peak, and Ross saw the figure slide limply from the saddle as the horse reared again.

He ran forward a few steps, searching for the other one. The rider squalled his fear, and Ross saw his arm rise and fall as he tried to lash the horse free. The horse took a bucking jump, and wire tightened about its legs. Ross heard the ripping of the wire through the brush as the animal's plunge took up slack. He fired in the instant before the horse fell, and the bullet slammed the rider from his seat. One horse was down, rolling and kicking in the wire. The other was still on its feet, plunging first one way, then another, the wire jerking each convulsive lunge up short.

Ross heard a shot from the front of the cabin and turned and ran that way. He yelled, "Enoch," marking himself as he ran. He did not want Redford turning and firing at the sound of new movement. He reached Redford, and the old man was panting with excitement.

"Two of them, Ross. I knocked one of them out of the saddle. The other's horse went down before I could get a shot at him. He's caught out there. Hear him?"

Ross listened to the man's swearing. There was a

frantic, desperate quality to the tone. Pain and terror made the man oblivious to the fact he had been fired upon.

"I'll take him," Ross said and glided forward.

The swearing stopped, but the sound of struggle still went on, acting as a signpost. The clouds parted, and the moon flooded the scene with light. Redford's shot was accurate, for a huddled form lay on its side. A horse rolled in the loose wire, hopelessly entangled. A loop of the stuff had tightened about its forelegs, making it impossible for it to get to its feet. A man stood near it, half crouched, his hands frantically plucking at the steel web. His hands made a lifting motion, then a throwing one, and Ross saw the gleam of light reflect from the strand of wire the man was trying to throw from him.

The loop bounced back, slapping against the man's arms, and his swearing started again, a wild, jumbled stream of words.

"Mack," Ross roared, and straightened.

The man turned clumsily, his movements hampered by the loops of wire wrapped about his body. There were dark, smeared lines along Mack's face where the wire had cut him, and his hands were covered with blood.

His head thrust forward as he recognized Ross, and a desperate cry burst from his mouth. He fumbled for his gun, but the wire was a restraining bond. Ross shot him before the hand was fully clasped about the pistol butt. The bullet plowed into his chest, and for an instant, Mack seemed to grow taller under its impact. Then he shriveled suddenly, falling in a loose heap.

Ross shot the threshing horse, and he regretted that more than the shooting of the men. Even with wire pliers it would have been dangerous trying to cut the horse loose; those kicking, lashing hoofs could scatter his brains.

He went back to Redford and said, "Just four of them, Enoch. Go tell Lynn it's all right."

He glanced at the lighted window of the cabin as he passed it. Lynn would be terrified, wondering at the meaning of all those shots.

He plodded to the rear of the cabin and dispatched the two horses there. He looked at the two dead men and recognized neither of them. Mack was the only one of the four he knew.

He walked back to the front of the cabin and squatted on his heels. He rolled a cigarette and pulled deep upon it. The smoke was hot and unsatisfying. His face was bleak as he stared at nothing. Tonight's violence would repulse Lynn, it would drive her even farther away. The thought had odd power to stab deep.

Redford came out and squatted beside him. He took the makings from Ross and said, "She's all right, I don't think she was as scared as I was." He licked the cigarette paper and twisted it. "I was scared and angry at the same time."

Ross asked, "Did you know any of them?"

Redford nodded. "One of them was out here this afternoon—the one you shot at and missed. I got him.

And you got Mack. I ain't looked at the other two yet."

Ross snapped away his cigarette. "Go look at them."

He scowled as Redford moved away. Mack would come here because of his hatred for Ross Stone. He would have no compunction at using help. If it hadn't been for the incident this afternoon, Ross could let it go at Mack's insane desire to kill him. But the two men had seemed unaware this afternoon that Ross was in the cabin.

Redford came back and said, "Never saw them before. Ross, Lynn wants to see you."

He wanted to see her too, and a dread pulled at him at the same time. He could not stand seeing revulsion in her face again.

He turned toward the cabin. The first look at her face would tell him where he stood.

Redford walked with him. He said, "Ross, you saw how helpless I was without you. Throw in with me. If somebody wants this piece of land this bad, we got a good thing."

Ross looked about him. If the property were as valuable as Redford suspected, he could work it for a while, and then follow the life he wanted. There was no reason why it should not be valuable. People all around them were taking wealth from the earth.

He blocked out that line of thinking and snapped, "I haven't got a dime, Enoch." His refusal was in his tone rather than in the words, and he heard Redford sigh.

Lynn waited just inside the cabin door, and he could read nothing in her face.

He said helplessely, "Lynn, there was no other way." Words were useless, and he flung up his hands in a helpless little gesture.

She said, "What would we have done, if it had not been for you?" Her voice was almost a wail. "Ross, can you understand what I'm trying to say?"

He wanted to, but he knew her words were prompted by gratitude. This moment's apparent softness would be gone all too soon. He thought of the man Redford had told him about, the man she had waited for.

He said gruffly, "You don't owe me any thanks, Lynn." She sensed the withdrawal in him, and her eyes were puzzled.

He said, "Lynn, I want you and Enoch to move into town. It's too lonely out here."

Her face went wooden. She said, "All right, Ross."

He wanted to reach out and draw her into his arms, but he wouldn't take advantage of her softness.

Chapter Twelve

GRAHAM said, "Jesus!" in a soft ejaculation. He cut his eyes at Lynn and said, "Sorry, ma'am." He looked back at Ross and shook his head. "Four of them."

"Five," Ross said shortly. "You're forgetting the one who was left this afternoon." He was tired and irritable. The trip into town had been a silent one, magnifying the distance out of all proportion.

"And they were all strangers to you?" Sheriff Graham peered suspiciously at Ross.

"I told you I'd seen Mack before," Ross snapped. "The rest were strangers."

"But you expected them," Graham said gloomily. "You were ready for them."

"We were ready for them," Ross said. His eyes bored into Graham's. He had told everything he knew about the entire affair, holding back nothing. Let Graham build whatever he could with it. He wanted to look at Lynn, but now that she had time to reflect upon what had happened, to be part of its aftermath, he was almost afraid to. In retrospect, five dead men was a big number.

She said passionately, "Don't we have the right to protect ourselves?"

Ross almost grinned in his relief. The anger was still with her. She was not thinking about numbers at all.

Graham sighed wearily. "You do. Don't any of you try to leave town. I want to talk to you more about this."

Lynn's face was still stormy. She started to say something, and Ross touched her arm. "Sheriff," he said. He kept all the animosity from his tone. He wanted a favor. "Lynn and Enoch can't go back there tonight. Do you know a place they can stay?"

Graham stared at him for a long moment, then reached for his hat. "I might get them in at Mrs. Mizner's. It's right around the corner. You wait for me here."

It was a direct order, and Ross asked, "You arresting me?"

"You stay here," Graham said stubbornly.

He took Redford's and Lynn's arm and steered them toward the door. She looked at Ross before she stepped outdoors. It was an odd look, one that he could not quite interpret. The quicker he got the Redfords out of his mind, the better off he would be. The same went for finding Cleve. He knew both things were going to take considerable doing.

Graham was back within a quarter of an hour. Ross was staring moodily at the floor. "They're all right," Graham said. "She's quite a girl."

"Yes," Ross said shortly.

Graham sat down, "You ain't told me how you got those marks on your face."

He stared steadily at Ross, and Ross grinned bleakly. He didn't blame Graham. In his place, he would be doing the same kind of probing. He said, "Mack put them there." He told Graham how it had started, of the first and second fight with him.

Graham's face was thoughtful. "Then he came after you. That part fits him. Mack was a bully. The Redfords got caught in the crossfire." He sighed and said, "But that doesn't explain the rest of them. What were they doing out there?"

"They were with Mack," Ross snapped.

"He wasn't that popular," Graham said sourly. He leaned forward, his eyes hard and insistent. "You ain't told me why you came here."

"It's still personal business," Ross said evenly. He pushed to his feet and said, "You holding me?"

"I knew you were trouble, when I first looked at you," Graham said moodily. "I ain't holding you now, but I want to see you in the morning."

"Sure," Ross said and turned toward the door. There was no spring in his legs, and his feet were heavy. Lord, he was tired. He could feel Graham's eyes upon him until he was out of sight.

He went to the livery stable and picked up his bedroll. It took him a long time to get comfortable. His side ached under the bandage Lynn had put on. He lay there, staring at the sky. Maybe time would help him get her out of his thoughts.

A shaft of sunlight awakened him in the morning. He blinked against it, then sat up. He tugged his boots on, yawned, and stretched. The sun was high, and from a nearby street he heard the rumble of a wagon. He had a long stretch of sleep behind him. He stood up and winced. He still had assorted twinges. He stepped outside and narrowed his eyes against the strengthening sun. He would keep one thought in mind until he was finished here. The first step was to find Cleve.

He gulped breakfast, then checked the livery stables and talked to three of the stage drivers without learning anything. The worry showed on his face as he walked to Graham's office. He was blocked every way he turned, and he could do nothing until he heard from Cleve.

Graham raised his head as Ross walked in and watched him with tired, thoughtful eyes. He said, "We brought them in this morning. Five dead men is a wagonload. It made quite a stir."

Ross remained silent. Let Graham do the leading.

"That damned wire gave us hell cutting through it. You were really set up for them."

"I told you that," Ross pointed out.

"What did you come here for?" Graham asked flatly.

Ross's tone matched his. "They had nothing to do with it."

"Maybe," Graham murmured.

Ross was tempted to tell him the whole story, then decided against it. You didn't tell a lawman you came to his town to kill a man.

Graham asked, "Did you find your brother?" His tone said, If there *is* a brother.

Anger came to life in Ross. "Why don't you ask your questions in the right directions? Who were those men? Who did they work for?"

Graham's face was heated. "You trying to tell me my business?" He hated to admit that he had never seen two of those five men before, that he knew Jude and Rezin only by sight and had no idea of their connections. Mack drove a stage for Tanner. He cursed silently.

"I know who Mack works for," Ross said.

"I already talked to Tanner." Graham's tone showed he was still ruffled. "He doesn't know anything about it. He says that if Mack had a personal score with you, he'd try to settle it. He's sorry about the whole thing." He paused, glaring angrily. "Don't you try pushing Tanner around."

"A big man?" Ross asked softly.

Graham glared at him. "He's never been on the wrong side of anything. Because he's grown rich is no reason—" He broke off, angry at himself for the explanation. "I'm warning you," he said flatly. "I've taken all the trouble I'm going to from you."

"Sure," Ross said and turned toward the door. Graham wasn't holding him, but from Graham's manner it seemed a very temporary condition.

Valerie threw the empty powder box across the room. Zachary had forgotten to bring her powder last night. How did he expect her to keep beautiful without the necessary supplies? She leaned forward to inspect her face in the mirror. She did not have enough powder to fully cover the scar where the mole had been. Zachary said the scar did not show, but she knew it was there. She had preferred the mole, for it caught men's eyes. It had been more of a beauty mark than a disfigurement. She was going to have to do something about her hair, for the line of blonde color at the roots was getting quite noticeable. She hated her hair black. She would be happy when Zachary let it grow back to its original blonde loveliness.

She studied her features, asking herself a question. Would Ross know her, if he saw her? She didn't think so. Two years was a long time, and on top of that, there were the changes in her appearance. She could think of him without the panic she had known when Zachary had first told her Ross was here. Perhaps it was the boredom that dissipated the panic, but confinement to this house was like being in jail. She arose from the dressing table and paced a restless turn about the room. Zachary was being overcautious. It wouldn't hurt to let her step outside for a breath of air. She thought of him with mixed emotions. She never denied that she loved him, but underlying currents also pulled at her. At times she was afraid of him, and others she almost hated him. But when he touched her the underlying currents vanished, and only her need of him remained. He had promised to spend the afternoon with her, and it was almost gone. She said petulantly, "Damn him!"

The boy came into the room and said, "Mummy, why can't I go outdoors and play?"

She whirled on him, her features setting with anger. "Because I said you couldn't." She saw the hurt on his face and was sorry. Her nerves were stretched thin, and she was taking it out on Chris.

She held out her arms and said, "Come here, darling." She held him tightly until he struggled against her embrace. She let him go and tried to make her voice light. "You can go out pretty soon, darling. Mummy thinks it best we stay inside for a while."

He said, "I want to go out now."

She restrained her rising anger. The stubborn streak was becoming more pronounced in him. In so many ways he was like Ross. He had Ross's coloring and the same general features. Two years had made a great change in Chris. He seemed to have doubled in height, and he had a trick of looking gravely at her as though he could see inside her. Ross used to do that, too.

A different sort of panic touched her. She didn't want to lose Chris. She said, "Aren't you happy here, Chris?" Those two years of flight had been hard on him. A child needed roots, a sense of security.

Chris considered the question before he answered. "Yes," he said. "But now I would like to go outside."

She laughed and pulled him close again. She was not going to lose him, ever. In his way, Zachary loved the boy, though at times they clashed, due to the increasing stubbornness in Chris. She felt an over-whelming desire to shelter Chris, and her arms tight-ened about him.

His voice sounded smothered as he asked plain-tively, "Why can't I go out?"

She held him at arm's length and said in a breathless rush, "We will go out, Chris. We'll go to the store and come right back." She looked out the window, and the twilight was fading. It would be dark in another few minutes. She said, "Chris, you won't tell Daddy about it."

Her exasperation returned with the time he took to answer her. Did he consider Zachary his daddy; did he ever remember Ross? Who could ever tell what a child was thinking?

He said, "I won't tell." The conspirator's glow in his eyes matched hers.

She said, "Get your cap."

She listened to him running through the other room and smiled. This imprisonment was hard on him. She turned to the mirror and adjusted a heavy veil about her face. She pinned on her hat and looked at herself. Ross would never recognize her, even if chance sent him her way. Would he recognize Chris? Her breath caught at the thought. Then she pushed it aside. She would not let fear dampen this little excursion.

She breathed deeply as she went down the street. Her confidence increased with each step. Not a head turned for a second look at a veiled woman and a small boy.

She hesitated at the door of the store. The place was crowded, and she knew how much Miller disliked children in his store. She saw him as he rushed from counter to shelf to table, attempting to wait on half a dozen people at once. He was a paper-thin man with sourness deep in his eyes. She was suddenly sorry that she had come, and she wanted to be waited upon and return home as quickly as possible. She would take no chance at additionally antagonizing Miller, and she said, "Chris, wait for me here on the porch."

He nodded his head, the shared gaiety between them gone.

She found her powder and picked up a box, hoping that Miller would wait on her. He pushed by her, his arms laden, and she dared not stop him. She knew if she interrupted him he would only make her wait longer.

She moved to the window, keeping one eye on

Miller and the other on Chris. The light from the window reached the boy at the railing. His back was toward her, his attention absorbed by the traffic passing before him. Her love for him was a tight knot, welling up in her throat. She should take him something, perhaps a sack of candy. Her face brightened at the thought, and she turned toward the table where bags of hard candy were stacked.

From the corner of her eye she saw a big man on the walk before the porch. Her breathing stopped, and a cruel hand squeezed her heart. The man was staring at Chris, and she knew him instantly. Please, God, no! It was a silent thought but so forceful she was sure everyone in the store was aware of it. One hand was pressed tightly against her throat, and she swayed dizzily. Ross Stone was retracing his steps toward the steps, his head still turned toward Chris.

She was frozen with terror, incapable of thought or action. She did not know the woman was near until she heard her voice. "What's the matter, dearie?" the woman asked. "Are you sick?"

Her voice was harsh, and there was equal harshness in her angular face, but her eyes were concerned.

Her words jolted Valerie's mind into frantic action. She looked back at the porch, and Ross was near Chris. As yet he had not spoken to the boy, for Chris's attention was still absorbed by something in the street. If she could only get Chris away before Ross questioned him.

She said in a frightened voice, "That man on the

porch. I'm afraid of him. If you could get my boy away from him and into the store—" She threw out her hand in an appealing gesture.

The woman said grimly, "One of that kind. The town is full of them. I'll get your boy away from him." She turned toward the door, determination in every angular line of her body.

Please, God, Valerie prayed. Let her get out there before Ross talks to him.

Ross moved along the walk, his movements as heavy as his thoughts. He was blocked every direction he turned, and the useless hours passing drove him wild. There was no trace of Cleve, or of Anson and Valerie. The trail apparently ended in Virginia City. He was up against a blank wall.

A segment of light from the store ahead of him flooded the walk. He moved through it; then his head turned, his attention focusing sharply on the boy behind the porch railing. His throat felt hot and dry, and his breathing came hard. The size looked about right, and the coloring was the same. How much did a boy change in two years?

He turned and moved toward the steps, his eyes never leaving the boy. If this were Chris, would Chris know him? Could a boy of five carry memories from two years back?

His voice came out dry and husky. He said, "Hello, son." The 'son' was an informal address, but he had hopes for it.

The boy turned his head and stared at him. A frown wrinkled his forehead. It could have meant anything, a puzzled trying to recall, or a resentment toward being disturbed.

Ross hunkered down until his head was on a level with the boy's. Did he really see something familiar in the boy's features, or did he just imagine it?

Ross ran his tongue around the inside of his mouth and asked, "You live here long, son?"

The boy stared at him with equal intensity, and a breathless exultation was beginning to sweep through Ross. He knows me, he thought. He's digging back, trying to place me.

"A long time," the boy said.

The sickening disappointment flooded in, making Ross's mind dull. Then the thought came, clear and sharp, a few months could be a long time to a boy. He could ask one question and know immediately. He could ask the boy's name. He moistened his lips before he spoke.

"Do you know me, son?" he asked instead.

Before the boy could answer a woman swept out onto the porch. She seized the boy's hand and said, "You come with me. Right now."

She did not give the boy time for argument. She pulled at his arm, and he followed her. He turned his head at the door and gave Ross a long, puzzled look before the woman jerked him inside.

Ross sat on his heels, his face blank. For an instant he felt he had been close to Chris, and the feeling was wrong. That was the boy's mother who commanded him with such authority, and she looked nothing like Valerie. This was the disappointment he knew so well, but this time it was more sickening. He shook his head and straightened, and his movements were tired and heavy. He stared out into the street, and he didn't see the woman take the boy to Valerie; he did not see Valerie hurry toward the store's rear door, pulling the boy after her.

He kept telling himself his feeling was wrong, but it persisted. That woman didn't have to be the boy's mother. He had jumped to a conclusion, and his feeling said it was wrong. He turned toward the door, knowing that he was probably letting himself in for more disappointment, but he had to talk to her.

She came out before he reached the door, and she was alone. He moved to intercept her, and she glared at him.

"Ma'am," he said, touching his hat. "Could I talk to you?"

Her hostility was as apparent as a club, and he wondered at it. "Ma'am," he said doggedly. "Was that boy your son?"

"You know he's not," she snapped. "And if you don't quit bothering her, you'll be sorry."

His feeling was right. He seized her arm and said hoarsely, "Where is she? Is she inside?"

She struck at his hand, and her face was furious. "There's law to stop men like you," she said. "You let her alone." He dropped her arm and turned toward the door, ignoring her clawing at him. Valerie and Chris were inside.

He stepped inside the store, his eyes going from face to face. He saw neither Valerie or Chris. He moved to the man in the soiled apron and caught his arm. "Mister," he asked. "Did you see a woman with a boy?" His hand measured a height. "About this tall?"

"Damn it," the man snapped. "I see a lot of women with kids. The store's full of them."

He started away, and Ross said, "They were in here just a couple minutes ago."

The man said, "I'm busy."

Heads were turning their way, and Ross let him go. His eyes swept over the room again, and he saw the rear door. He hurried to it, opened the door, and stepped into an alley. He looked one way, then the other. She had only a few minutes' start, but which way did she go?

He briefly turned his head at the store owner's angry shout. The man stood framed in the doorway, and he yelled, "You stay out of my store." The banging door gave emphasis to his words.

Ross ran down the alley toward the west. He came out of it onto a street filled with traffic. It would have been a simple matter for her to mingle with the crowd and become lost. The other end of the alley fed onto an equally busy street. He might not find her tonight, but the doubts were gone. She was here, and he had seen his son. Cleve's letter was right. The trail ended here in Virginia City. Ross still had to find them, but with the uncertainties gone, it was only a matter of time. A child was hard to keep hidden. People noticed children more than they did grown-ups. Now it was a matter of looking at every boy in Virginia City. It would take time, but he would willingly spend it. For he had seen his son. Chris's face was very vivid before his eyes.

Chapter Thirteen

A T THE END of the next day, Ross had seen two dozen boys of assorted sizes and ages. Each had a certain appeal, but none of them was Chris. He had asked questions of them, describing Chris as he remembered him last night, and the results were the same as his search for Cleve. None of them had a playmate like Ross described.

He shook his head as he thought of Cleve. Finding Cleve would have to wait; he could take care of himself. Chris was a different matter. If necessary, he would look into every house in the city.

He did not realize he was walking by Mrs. Mizner's boarding house until he was almost past the building. He quickened his stride, not wanting to talk to the Redfords, particularly Lynn. Then he heard her call. Reluctantly he stopped and turned.

She came toward him, a smile on her face, and he could not look at it long. It reminded him of the loss of many things.

She said, "Ross, I've been thinking about you all day."

"Yes?" His word held no encouragement for her.

Her smile weakened but still remained on her face. "Will you eat with us tonight?"

He shook his head. She mixed up his thinking: she weakened his resolution.

Her smile disappeared, and her face went strained. "All right, Ross. You'd rather die in your hate then come back to life. You were hurt, but that was in the past. No one can live there." Her voice rose a note. "Do you think you're the only one who has ever been hurt?"

He said flatly, "She took my son with her. It's more than just hate. I want my son back."

She said flatly, "Perhaps he would rather be with his mother."

Anger was beginning in his eyes. She had a perverse streak that always took the opposite side. "He had no choice," he growled.

She said, "Oh, Ross. And you'd spend the rest of your life searching for them. If you haven't found them after two years—"

"I saw Chris last night," he said.

She stared at him, and he saw pity and disbelief in her eyes.

"I saw him," he repeated.

"Did he know you?" Her voice was very low.

"I didn't get but a minute to talk to him. But it was Chris."

She shook her head and said, "Don't you see, Ross. You've been filled with a single idea for so long that—"

"You think I'm imagining things, that I see Chris in every boy I look at." His anger had hold of him, and he wanted to hurt her. "I'll take care of my own affairs, Lynn."

She stared at him and said, "You will, I know, regardless of whom it hurts. Good-by, Ross."

He watched her move away and wanted to call her back, but she was only an added complication, and he was afraid of it. He turned and headed rapidly for the nearest saloon.

Tanner stood just inside the door that led to the main room of the saloon. He nervously chewed his lower lip as he watched the growing crowd. A week ago, the sight of that money pouring into his place would have given him extreme pleasure. Now, the thought of losing it was torture. Damn Ross Stone. Tanner checked his thoughts. He had to keep a constant hand on the wildness that threatened to overwhelm him. Who would have believed it possible that Stone could kill all four of them? But it was true; Graham had said so. Who would he send after him now? All over town men were talking in awed tones about Stone. It would take a large sum of money to send anyone else after him, and that would tie him in. He couldn't risk that, and he couldn't let Stone remain alive.

You could go yourself, a mocking inner voice said. Tanner shuddered at the thought. He could not face Stone; he could not even attempt to shoot him from ambush. There was always the chance of missing, a chance too big to take. He had to think. He knew why he was standing here; he was watching the front door. If Stone came in, Tanner was prepared to flee out the back door.

He saw the head and shoulders appear above the swinging doors, and the sucking hollow in his stomach threatened to engulf him. Was Stone's coming here only chance, or was there deliberate purpose in him?

The doors swung open, and Stone entered. He didn't look around as if searching for someone; he headed straight for the bar, looking as though he wanted nothing more than a drink.

Tanner backed away from the door and wiped his damp face. That could be crafty purpose in Stone's attitude, but he had to accept it for what it seemed to be. It might be best if he walked out there and tested Stone's ability to recognize him. But he couldn't do it. Instead, he hurried to his office, wanting a shut door between himself and Stone.

He sat at his desk for what seemed an eternity, listening to the muted noises from below. These were friendly noises, sounds he was used to, but tonight each held an alien note. What was Stone doing? Was he coming up the stairs, was he now standing outside the door?

He jerked at the knock on the door; then the knock was repeated, and a woman's voice called, "Zachary, let me in."

He recognized Susie's voice, moved to the door and

unlocked it. She came into the room, his frown not deterring her.

He said testily, "Susie, I'm busy. What is it?"

Her eyes searched his face, and he had the feeling she could see through him. "What's troubling you, Zachary?" she asked. "I could help, if you'd let me."

He wanted to swear at her; he wanted to slap her across the room, but he managed a smile and said, "Nothing's troubling me, Susie."

"I could be nice to you, if you'd let me," she murmured.

He turned her toward the door. "I'll keep it in mind, Susie. But now you'd better get back to business."

Her eyes were cold before she shut the door. "Some day you might need me, Zachary."

His smile was a grimace, and it held until the door closed behind her. There was a threat in her words which he didn't miss. She was a threat as long as she knew about Cleve. If she ever got together with Stone—Tanner shuddered as he stared at the door.

Ross walked to the bar and said, "Whisky." He waited until the bartender poured the glassful and said, "Leave the bottle." He pulled out some coins and shoved them across the bar.

Ross moodily drank glass after glass. He liked a shot of whisky after a long day or a cold one, but he had never been in the hard-drinking class. Now he was willing that the whisky sponge out his thinking, but regardless of how hard he punished the bottle, he kept seeing Lynn's face and hearing her words. He had been a damned fool. She was offering him something, and he had driven her off.

He pushed the bottle away when there was only a third of it left. He jerked his hat over his eyes and turned toward the door. With his first step, his knee buckled, and he lurched.

He straightened and glared about to see who was watching him. He felt mean and lonesome. He growled to himself and moved unsteadily toward the street. The evening traffic bumped and jostled him. A hand fastened on his arm, and he whirled, full of fight. The fight disappeared as he looked at the woman standing in the doorway. For an instant he thought it was Lynn, and his heart lurched. He recognized her then. Her name was Ida, Ida something.

He said flatly, "It's you."

She smiled faintly. "That isn't the most complimentary thing I've heard."

Three men passed down the walk, and the inside one bumped Ross. The impact staggered him. The pressure of her hand increased, pulling him into the building. "You're drunk," she said.

"I am, like hell," he growled.

"You're giving a good imitation of it," she said cheerfully. "Come on. I'll add some fuel to the fire." She tugged on his arm, and he followed her into the big room.

He blinked against the dazzle of the overhead lamps. He felt the thickness of the carpet under his boots, and the red plush settees, lining the walls, looked soft enough to swallow a man. Half a dozen girls were primping before a big mirror.

"The evening hasn't started yet," Ida said. A faint smile was on her lips as she watched him.

The women turned from the mirror, their eyes boldly going over him. In this elegance and with all those eyes upon him, he was aware of his worn, soiled clothing. He grinned in embarrassment and rubbed his knuckles along his beard stubble.

One of the women took a couple of steps forward and dropped her handkerchief.

"Tillie," Ida said sharply.

Tillie straightened, and her face was sullen. "Doesn't he get a choice?" she asked boldly. Ida locked eyes with her, and Tillie looked away first. "All right," she said sullenly. "All right."

Ida smiled at Ross, but her eyes were still angry. "Sometimes the girls are hard to manage," she said lightly.

She steered him toward a door on the other side of the room. She opened it and looked back. Every eye in the room was upon them. She looked at Ross, and her smile was mocking. "They can't believe it," she said. "This doesn't often—" She shrugged and let the remainder of the words die.

She looked at one of the women and said, "Bess. Take over." Her smile was enigmatic, "for awhile."

She led him down a corridor with doors on each side of it. She opened a door at the end of the hall, and he felt more out of place than ever. The room screamed femininity. Those were real lace curtains at the window, and a flounced spread was on the bed.

"Come on, come on," she said impatiently and led him into the room.

He sat down in one of the easy chairs beside the bed and sprawled his legs out before him, staring at the toes of his worn boots. The whisky was like a fog, swirling and closing in on his thoughts, but one thought struck clearly through the murk.

"Why, Ida?" he asked.

She shrugged again. Her shoulders were round and soft above the low cut of her gown and particularly mobile. The lamplight in here was kind, softening her face. It was not often she asked herself that question any more. She could not truly answer why, but she felt a strange eagerness, the same eagerness she had known when she touched him the night of the fight. How many men had she known in her life? She had no idea of the number. They were faceless men, with the exception of a few she could count on one hand. This man had a face, a face that stood out above even the few. From the first moment she had seen it, she had been struck by the loneliness in the eyes, by the restless seeking of them, and it had fired a responsive chord in her.

She said abruptly, "I was lonesome. I wanted someone to talk to." She smiled at his surprise. "You're thinking of the girls living here. Try living with a bunch of women and see how hungry you get for talk—real talk."

He grinned. It was comfortable being here. She was the type one felt instantly at ease with. He squinted at her and thought, she's more handsome than I remembered.

She moved to a table, poured two small glasses of brandy from a bottle sitting there and came back. She placed one of them in his hand and traced a finger along the line of his jaw.

"Don't gulp that," she said. "That's good brandy."

He took the brandy in small sips, feeling the warmth of it spreading throughout his body. It combined forces with the whisky, and the two of them packed an awful wallop.

She filled his glass each time it was empty, and she matched him glass for glass. It kept getting a firmer grip on him, and he knew his talk was becoming rambling and disjointed. But it didn't matter; it didn't seem to have any effect upon her, except that her eyes grew bigger and more luminous. He didn't need any other woman as long as she was here. The fog was thicker in his mind, and the room didn't seem as bright as it had.

He asked querulously, "You turn out some of the light?"

She leaned close to him, and he could feel the fan of her breath against his face. Her smile seemed enormous. "You're drunk, Ross," she said. "You'd better lie down."

He didn't remember lurching toward the bed; he didn't remember her tugging off his boots.

• • •

He awakened in the morning, and it took him a long moment to remember where he was. He stared at the ceiling, then at the far wall, then had the feeling someone was beside him. He carefully turned his head to keep the pounding in it at a minimum. She lay beside him, her head turned watching him, and only a sheet covered her, outlining her pointed breasts.

He said hoarsely, "Hell, Ida. Did I—" His tongue swelled in his mouth, and he could not complete the question.

He didn't remember, but she did. She had lain awake most of the night listening to his disjointed talk. Even after he had fallen asleep, she had watched him. She had taken a segment of his life and built it into her own, and she was a wise enough woman never to ask more than that segment.

"You did," she said and chuckled at the expression on his face.

She sat up, and the sheet fell away from her. He saw the white and coral of her breasts before she bent over him. She kissed him hard, then lay back. She did not bother to cover herself again. She said, "Don't think about it." She did not expect him to, but she would. At odd times, the night would come floating back.

He saw his pants lying on a chair beside the bed and pulled them on. He stood up and said awkwardly, "Did I make a fool of myself?"

She shook her head in violent disagreement. For an

149

instant, she rebelled at how fleeting the moment was, then the rebellion was gone.

She said, "You talked. I know why you came to Virginia City."

He looked at her, his face perturbed.

"You talked about Anson and Valerie and the boy. And you talked about Cleve." He had also talked about Lynn, but she would not tell him that.

He slipped into his shirt and buttoned it, his face grim. "They're here. I don't know what's happened to Cleve. But I saw Chris last night." She did not question his statement as Lynn had done, and he was relieved.

"What are you going to do?"

He said harshly, "I'm going to look at every boy in Virginia City."

"Finding her would be just as good?"

He nodded again. If he found Valerie, he would find Chris.

"I might help you find her."

He sat down on the edge of the bed and tugged on his boots. He asked, "How?" The question was full of doubts.

She thought of how she could pull him back here time and time again, then she dismissed the idea. She would not put a price on her help.

She smiled and said, "You'd laugh at what I have in mind. But I know women. It could work. I'll find you when I know something. Tell me how I can recognize her."

He described Valerie in detail, and as she listened to him she thought how often a man remembers so well a woman who has hurt him. And the others he can not recall at all. From his description she knew a great deal about Valerie. If she were still in Virginia City, Ida thought she could be drawn out of hiding.

He said, "Thanks again, Ida." He bent down and kissed her, a kiss with no passion. He touched her cheek with his fingers, then strode out of the room.

Chapter Fourteen

AT THE END of two days Ross's determination was weakening. He had been met with suspicion, rebuff and hostility. It was getting increasingly difficult to knock on a door and ask the woman, who answered it, "Ma'am, do you have any children? May I see them?" He needed someone to talk to. Lynn was not sympathetic. There was Ida, but he was reluctant to go there again.

He turned toward the nearest saloon. It was the same one he had been in the other night, but one saloon was like another. It wasn't a drink so much he wanted as companionship. He saw a bearded man start at his entrance, then turn abruptly and hurry toward a rear door. He wondered about the man's haste, then dismissed it.

He moved to the bar, pushing through the crowd. The place was thronged as was every place in Virginia City after dark, and the hot, stale air lay in heavy layers. He listened to the talk on every side of him and knew a sense of being completely shut off.

He felt eyes upon him and slowly turned his head. A faded woman was intently watching him. From her dress, he thought she worked here. She was evidently seeking an invitation, and he was not interested. He looked back at the bar and saw her in the mirror.

He ordered a drink to keep his place at the bar and slowly turned the glass in his hand, watching the amber liquid. This was no good. He was accomplishing nothing here, and still he was reluctant to leave the lights and talk.

Graham pushed against the bar beside him and growled, "I want to talk to you."

Ross half turned his head. That was open hostility on Graham's face. He said, "Yes?" in a toneless voice.

'I got a half-dozen complaints about you this afternoon," Graham said explosively. "What the hell are you doing now?"

Ross asked bleakly, "Who complained?" He thought he knew. Some of those mothers had been indignant at his questions.

"You know who complained," Graham snapped. "What are you after?"

Ross' tone hardened to match Graham's. "It's still personal business," he said.

Graham said bitterly, "You won't go around bothering people, while I have a say. I'm warning you. If I get one more complaint about you, I'm arresting you."

"On what charges?" Their heated controversy was

drawing attention. Ross saw a dozen heads turned their way.

"Disturbing the peace." Graham's eyes were hot coals.

Ross said flatly, "I'll keep it in mind." He left the bar and pushed through the crowd. The wildness was rising. He was blocked every way he turned.

Tanner ran up the stair and into his office. He closed the door behind him and leaned against it to steady his shaky knees. He had not been here for two days, and the moment he came in, Stone followed him. Did it mean something, or was it more happenstance?

He sat down at the desk, his teeth clenched against the shaking of his jaws. Everything was falling apart and because of one man. Even Valerie was different the last two days. She acted as though some tremendous strain had touched her, and she denied it, when he questioned her. She wanted to leave Virginia City, but he could not leave on the spur of the moment like this; he could not run and leave all his assets. He needed a little time in which to convert them into money.

Tanner jumped at the knock. He grabbed a gun in each hand and leveled them on the door. "Who is it?" he called.

"Susie. Let me in."

His face twisted with rage. He did not want to see her or talk to her now. He started to yell at her to get away from that door, then thought better of it. She had been downstairs, she would know if Stone was still here.

He laid the pistols on the desk and crossed to the door. He unlocked it and opened it wide enough to admit her. He closed it behind her and tried to make his breathing normal. She watched him with veiled eyes.

She looked at the pistols on the desk, and her eyes grew mocking. "Zachary, you haven't been very nice to me. I kept waiting for you to change, but you didn't. You will now."

He said in a rasping voice, "Shut up, Susie."

Her eyes were twin chips of ice. "I'll talk, and you'll listen. I don't have to beg for your favor. Not any more, I don't. You're going to do the begging now."

He said savagely, "Why, you damned fool." He strode across the room and struck her. Her head rocked back, and she bit her lip, but she made no outcry. She moved to the door. She turned her head, and her eyes blazed at him. "That's all I needed. I could have loved you. You're going to be sorry." Her face turned ugly as she spat the words at him.

He yelled, "Get out of here."

Her lips curled with contempt. "You're scared, Zachary. And I know who you're scared of. It's the big man who just came in. I saw your face, when you looked at him. I saw you run twice from him. Is he connected with the man you had tied in this room? Mack showed me all the, money he had. You're the one who paid him to try to kill the big man. He killed Mack, and he'll kill you."

Her words froze him with shock, then his face went insane. "Susie," he shouted. "Come here."

His look turned her face white. She should never have told him how much she guessed. She flung open the door and ran down the hall. Her heart kept climbing into her throat, impeding her breathing. She heard the clatter of his boots behind her.

As crazy as he looked, he would not dare do anything to her with all the people in the saloon watching him.

Tanner checked his stride halfway down the stairs. Even though he owned this place, fifty men would stop him, if he laid a hand on her. He remembered he left his pistols on the desk, but there was no time to go back for them. He had to keep her in sight. He leaned over and touched the knife in its boot sheath. It would be enough.

His breathing was under control by the time he reached the bottom of the stairs. He passed the end of the bar, and the bartender said, "What's wrong with Susie? She went through here like she was shot out of a gun."

Tanner's elaborate shrug said Who knows why a woman does anything? He sauntered through the room, when every fiber of his being demanded haste. He could not let her get out of sight. He could not let her carry her suspicions to Ross Stone or even Graham.

He stepped outside and looked down the street. It was going to be hard to see her in the crowd. He let out an explosive puff of relief. He saw her hurrying across the street.

He fell in a half block behind her, content to keep her in sight for now. He could do nothing as long as she was surrounded by people.

He followed her for a block, then stopped short. Stone was talking to a group of men, and she was heading straight for that group. His breathing clogged in his throat again. He longed for a gun. He pressed tight against a building wall. All she had to do was to point a finger, and Stone would have his fresh trail.

Chapter Fifteen

Ross moved up the street, thinking of Graham's words.

Graham meant every word he said, and Ross was up against a hard wall. A sense of helplessness engulfed him. He had enough against him without adding the law.

Three men were standing on the corner, ahead of him, and one of them stopped him, asking for a match. "Not a gol-durned one of us has a light," the man said.

Ross fished out several matches. He accepted the makings and rolled a cigarette, welcoming this break in the churning of his thoughts.

The matches went around, and the men puffed in silence.

The white-haired one said, "You don't look like no miner."

"I'm not," Ross said. His reply sounded abrupt. He had lost the gift of small, easy conversation. To amend the abruptness he said, "It looks like better cattle country to me."

"It is," the man said vehemently. "When people get through scratching around, that's what it'll be. Don't you ever let this mining get a hold on you."

"It won't," Ross said. He thought of Redford's tentative offer. If he had the money and nothing else on his mind, he might consider it. But only long enough to get bigger money for a new start in ranching. He thought of Lynn and of how she added in his already tangled affairs. He said to break the silence, "It's good country."

"It shore is," the white-haired man replied.

Susie kept looking back over her shoulder, and the sense of terror diminished as she did not see Tanner. Damn him. He would worry. She wondered if she had been foolish, for now she could not go back. She lifted her head in a defiant gesture. She did not want to go back. There were other places, and she was tired of Virginia City. But before she left she was going to make him pay, if she could.

She thought of the facts she knew about him and saw how thin they were. She checked each item off in her mind, and singledly or collectively none of them stood for much. She had seen a look of fear on his face and a hasty ducking, when the big man entered the saloon. That was really all she had to go on. She frowned as she walked down the street. But how could he explain his violent reaction when she spoke of it to him? She wished she knew who the big man was and where she could find him.

Then she saw the man she wanted, up ahead, talking to three others. She quickened her step and thought, We'll see, Zachary Tanner.

Ross did not know she was near until she touched his sleeve. He turned as she said, "Please. May I talk to you?"

He stared at her, a little frown creasing his forehead. He had seen this woman before, but he could not place her. She had the hard stamp of the dance-hall girl, and he thought, that was it. He had seen her in one of the saloons. He touched the brim of his hat and said, "Yes, Ma'am?"

She looked at the big rugged man. She could not talk before all these listening men. But he was waiting, a frown growing on his face.

She said in quick desperation, "Will you come to my room?" She saw the covert grins touching the other men's lips and the refusal forming on his face. She kept her indignation under control and said, "This could be important to you. You've been looking for something, haven't you?"

His eyes sharpened. "Yes," he said in a clipped tone. "What do you know about it?" Where had he seen this woman?

"My room is at the back of Miller's store. I'll be waiting for you."

He reached out a hand to detain her, and she shook her head. "If you're interested, you'll be there."

She moved quickly away and looked back after a dozen yards. He watched her, that frown still on his face. But he was interested; he would come. A sense of triumph flooded her. All right, Zachary, she thought. Now we'll see.

Ross turned her words over in his mind. Did she know something, or was this some new kind of an approach?

The white-haired man's words jarred him out of his thoughts. "That was something new," the man said. "I never did have one of them come up and tell me I was looking for something important. By golly, she's right. It's damned important." He put mock sorrow on his face. "Or it used to be."

The other two joined in, and their kidding was ribald. What did Ross have? He sure must keep it hidden, because it didn't show.

He accepted the raillery with outward good grace, but his thoughts were busy. He would wait a decent interval, five or ten minutes at least. He would not let them see how eager he was to talk to the woman.

Tanner watched the group of men in an agony of indecision, He saw Susie walk away from them, and he would have given a large sum of money to know what she said to Stone. It could not have been very much, for the time interval was too short. He kept his eyes riveted on Stone, awaiting some reaction, some indication that would tell him what to do. Stone went on talking to the men, appearing easy and relaxed.

Tanner's hopes quickened. Maybe she had said nothing definite to Stone, maybe she asked him to meet her someplace else.

He saw her turn the corner at Miller's store, and his eyes were hot and wicked. That was it. She would not talk before all of them, she expected Stone to come to her room.

His eyes switched back to the group. How much time did he have? He turned and darted around the block. He breathed hard as he came down the side street which her room faced. Stone would come from the opposite direction, and Tanner's breathing eased as he saw the street was empty. He approached the door of her room, his nerves drawn so fine they put a physical ache in him. Once inside her room, he could not be trapped, for there was a small back window he could use. She would be expecting Stone to knock, and Tanner drew a deep, steadying breath before he pulled the knife from its sheath. He held it in his right hand and rapped softly with his left.

He heard the sound of her footsteps, then the door opened a small crack. He shoved hard against it with his shoulder, knocking her back into the room. He was through the door in a leap, kicking it shut with his heel.

She stood in a sort of shock, her eyes wide and horrified, fixed on the naked blade. Her face blanched as her eyes rose to his face.

"Zachary," she whimpered. "I wasn't going to tell him anything." She retreated as he came toward her. "Zachary! You've got to believe me."

160

He reached her in a long stride. An arm wrapped around her head, and a hand clamped over her mouth. "You should have, Susie. You waited too long."

He caught a flash of her eyes, round and filled with entreaty as he raised the knife. It took all his strength to hold her with the one arm. Her hands clawed at him, and he felt fingernails rip one cheek. Her body arched away from him, and the sting of his torn flesh drove him wild. "You bitch," he said savagely.

He drew her back to him, ignoring the flailing hands. He plunged the knife between her breasts, then seized her with both hands. He held her erect in a tight grip until the last convulsive shudder left her body. He breathed hard as he lowered her to the floor. His hands were covered with bright crimson, and he stooped and wiped them on her dress. A slight shiver ran through him as he looked at her. A moment ago, she had been a kicking, struggling fury, and now she was nothing. It took such a short space of time to bring that about. He stared at her as though mesmerized. The knock on the door broke the spell. His eyes flicked to the door, then to the window. His breathing was harsh and hurting in his throat. He had taken the gamble and won. He crossed to the window on noiseless feet. It made a squeaking sound as he raised it.

Ross knocked on the door. There was no answer and the door was not opened. He stiffened as he heard a peculiar squeaking sound. It could come from a window being raised.

He knocked again, a louder, more demanding knock.

He waited a brief moment, then dropped his hand to the knob. It turned, engaging the catch, and his indecision lasted only a split-second before he opened the door. If she were not here, he could leave and no one would be the wiser.

The room was lit with a lamp, and for an instant, he did not see her. It was a cheaply furnished little room, pathetic in its attempt to be made livable. The air was heavy with the stale smell of perfume—and something else.

His eyes were drawn to her, and seeing her was a hard, numbing blow. She lay on her back, the knife haft standing erect. The front of her dress was dyed a brilliant red and the same color puddled on the floor beside her. He knew she was dead without touching her, but he leaned over and felt her arm. The flesh was warm to the touch. He straightened, and his eyes went to the window. He ran to it, drawing his gun. So it was a window he had heard being opened, and the murderer had gone through it only seconds before. His eyes swept the backyard, and he saw no movement. The murderer had had ample time to reach the corner.

Ross knew maddening frustration as he stared out into the night. The woman did have vital information for him—so vital that someone was fearful of her talking. Anson, or someone close to Anson, had been within reaching distance.

He turned from the window and put a last glance upon the woman. He felt pity, but there was nothing he could do for her. He could not even tell Graham she was dead; he could not let Graham know he had been here, for this time Graham would react with violence.

He crossed to the door and opened it. He peered out into the street, and it was empty. Someone would find her tomorrow. He closed the door and went quickly down the street. He would wait until the woman was found, then learn her background. From her background might come a sign pointing to the man who was afraid enough of her to murder her.

Chapter Sixteen

B Y NOON of the following day, Ross saw no unusual disturbance in the town. There would have been, if the woman had been found. Men would have clustered on every corner, excitedly talking about it. He had been by Graham's office half a dozen times, and there was no furor there.

He spent some time in watching the house in which the dead woman lay. No one beside himself showed any unusual interest. He dared not linger too long. After she was found, no one must remember his interest.

He turned from watching the house, his face heavy. Two fruitless days had been spent in looking for the boy. Should he abandon that phase of the search and concentrate on looking for the woman's killer? He shook his head, a heavy, almost defeated gesture. Each way he turned seemed to be blocked.

He came around a corner, and Lynn was coming

toward him. Her shoes were covered with dust, and there was a faint film of it on her face. She had been doing considerable walking, and he wondered why. She saw him, and her face brightened.

She said, "Ross," and hurried toward him. The brightness in her face faded as she saw the stiffness in his.

"Ross," she said, her eyes earnest. "You mustn't believe I didn't believe you, or that I thought you obsessed."

"What do you want me to believe?" he growled.

She took a deep breath, and her face paled, but her eyes were quite steady. "I wanted you to give up the search, Ross. I think I was afraid you would find them." She looked at him steadily. "Ross," she said with quick indignation. "Can't you understand what I'm saying?"

"I understand," he said, the heavy note back in his voice. "And I can do nothing about it." He put a crushing hand on the new life flaring inside him.

He saw her eyes dull and her shoulders droop. It was hard not to reach out a hand to her, for he knew now. He said. "Lynn, I love you. I guess I have almost from the first time I saw you."

The light came back to her eyes and there was a gladness in her face.

He did not want to wipe either away, but he had to. He said steadily, "Lynn, I'm still a married man."

"I know," she said with a rush of breath. "I'm not asking for anything. Just hearing what you said—"

She stopped and shook her head. Her eyes were misty, and there was a look on her face a man was not often privileged to see.

He said hoarsely, "Lynn," and reached out and took her hand. "I could have been mistaken the other night. It might not have been Chris at all. I promise you this. If they're not here, I'll look no farther. I'll give it up."

She squeezed his hand, and the pressure was surprisingly strong. "I think I was most afraid you'd be leaving again, Ross. I want you to do what you feel you have to."

That was all a man needed, the understanding and support of the woman he loved. He folded her hand in both of his and wished this damned street were empty.

She pulled her hand away after a long moment and said fiercely, "I want this over for you. Tell me what to do to help."

He recalled Graham's warning and said, "You can help me look, Lynn." He described the boy as he remembered from the other evening. "If you find him, let me know."

She searched his face and said, "You're after something else?"

"I don't know, Lynn," he said slowly. He told her of last night's happenings, ending with the finding of the woman. "She was killed to keep her from talking to me. If I can find the man who did it—" His eyes were hard as he stared off into space.

"Can't Graham help?"

He shook his head. "I don't dare go to Graham. He's

connecting me with everything that's happening around here. If he learns I was in this, the least he'll do is to throw me in jail. I wouldn't blame him. But he could keep me there for weeks while he runs around in circles."

She asked in a small voice, "The dead woman knew the man you're hunting?"

He nodded. "It's possible. He might have seen her talking to me, then killed her in fear that she would tell me more than she did." His voice grew bitter. "I was just a couple of minutes behind him. I heard the window open."

Her voice was a whisper. "There's only one thing I ask, Ross. Be careful."

"Sure," he said steadily. He plodded away from her and looked back after a dozen strides. She stood there, watching him. She was near enough to touch and yet a million miles away.

Valerie picked up the hand-bill, then threw it aside. She had read it a dozen times. She wanted to go to that sale, and it would be a foolish thing to do. But the walls of this house were beginning to close in about her. Her fright of two nights ago was abating, but enough of it remained to make her catch her breath every time she thought of it. She had begged Zachary to leave Virginia City, and he had refused. Did he think he could keep her penned up in this house forever? She picked up the hand-bill again. She had never heard of such prices. How much danger would there be in going to that sale? None, she argued with herself. There would be only women present.

Chris came into the room and asked, "Mummy, will I ever see that man again?"

He had asked that question a dozen times, and she wanted to scream at him. She kept her voice normal and said, "Chris, I told you to forget him. Why do you keep asking?" She had been terrified that he would ask the question while Zachary was around, and she must make him forget it.

She put her arms about him and said, "He means nothing to us, Chris. I want you to promise to forget him."

He shook his head, and she recognized the stubborn quality of the gesture. "Mummy, do I know him?" he asked.

She thought wildly, I can't stand anymore of this. She saw the hand-bill and thought, I'm going to that sale. Anything to get away from the searching regard in the boy's eyes.

She put on her hat and pinned on the veil. "Chris, Mummy's going out for awhile. I want you to promise me you won't leave the house until I get back."

His slowness to answer enraged, her, and she seized his arms. "Do you hear me?"

He said, "I'll stay."

That was almost dislike in his eyes, and the wildness grew in Valerie. Ross Stone was driving a wedge between them. Zachary had to kill him; he had to.

She said in a choked voice, "I'll be right back,

Chris." She looked back from the door. Chris watched her, the withdrawn look still in his eyes.

Ross moved back to the business section of town for more waiting and listening. The afternoon wore on and the streets grew hotter. Men sought the shadowy interiors of buildings looking for at least the illusion of coolness. The afternoon dragged away and Ross saw no break in the ordinary routine of the town.

The sun was low when Ida found him in front of the Wells Fargo station. Her face was flushed both from the heat and an inner excitement. She said, "I've been looking all over for you."

He remembered the night he had spent with her and knew a guilty twinge. He said uneasily, "Yes?"

If she felt his uneasiness, she did not comment upon it. She thrust a hand-bill at him and said, "Look!"

He frowned as he read the big printing on the bill. It announced a sale of women's dresses and hats, describing each item and giving its cost.

He handed back the bill. A woman might get excited over something like that, but it meant nothing to him. The uneasiness grew as he wondered if she expected him to buy her something. He felt his face heat. "Ida, I—"

She cut him short with an impatient gesture. "I donated most of those dresses myself. I paid the girls for the others. Don't you see? A sale like this will draw any woman. I had the hand-bills printed with prices no woman could resist. I had them distributed over town, and I think every woman here came."

He stared at her, and she nodded. Her voice held grim satisfaction. "Good women won't associate with us, but they'll buy our clothes at give-away prices. She came, Ross. She was heavily veiled, but she took off her hat to try on another one. She wasn't blonde, and there was no mole on her face, but it was her, all right."

The eagerness faded from his face. "It couldn't be her, Ida. I told you—"

Her laugh interrupted him. "I know what you told me. There was a scar on her cheek where the mole was, and her hair was blonde at the roots. A woman can spot dyed hair in a minute."

Words were hard to get through his tight throat. "You're sure, Ida?"

"I'm sure."

"You know where she went?"

"I followed her."

The end was before him, and he owed it to this woman. He gazed soberly at her and asked, "Ida, what can I do to make it up to you?"

For an instant, she had the wild thought of drawing him to her against his will. But she was intelligent enough to know that the hold would be only brief at best. She said, "You can make up the difference those clothes cost." She imagined she saw him wince and said, "Any time. There's no hurry." It meant she would see him again. She put the thought out of her mind. It meant nothing.

He asked slowly, "Where is she, Ida?"

She looked steadily at him. "You want to know?"

He nodded his head decisively. Lynn changed things enough for him to forget Valerie—but there was Chris. And Cleve. The name popped into his mind. Cleve was involved in this.

She gave him directions and said, "It's a big white house on the outskirts. It stands by itself at the end of the street."

She caught his arm as he started to move away. "Be sure, Ross."

"I am," he said.

She watched the broad shoulders move away, and an odd lump was in her throat. If that was the way he wanted it, she hoped she had helped him.

He walked down the street with deliberate strides. He could not say he was filled with hatred as he had once been. Perhaps the long months had burned most of it away. He knew eagerness to see Chris, but it was laced with dread at seeing her. He was not sure what he was going to say to her. He was only sure of one thing. He was going to take Chris from her—and make her tell about Cleve, if she knew anything.

He turned a corner, and a tall, bearded man came toward him. The man suddenly stopped and fumbled in his vest pocket. Ross watched him with detached curiosity. He saw him pull out a cigar and light it, and the bearded face was half shielded by the cupped hands. Ross noticed the scratches on the cheek that was turned toward him. They stood out in livid streaks, and he thought, it looks as though a woman clawed him. He forgot about the man as soon as he walked by him.

Tanner raised his head shakily. The trembling in his hands ceased. Stone had passed him in broad daylight and had not recognized him. He was safe, completely safe. Only one person in Virginia City knew of his past, and she would never talk. She had been pestering him to leave Virginia City, and now there was no need for it. He wanted to run the remaining distance to the house to tell her they were safe.

Ross walked on down the street, never varying his stride. A voice hailed him from across the street, and he turned his head.

He frowned as he saw Graham crossing to him. He decided Graham's manner showed no particular hostility. It would not hurt to exchange a few words with him. A little more delay would not matter.

Chapter Seventeen

TANNER knew a boundless exuberance as he walked toward his house. All the past nightmare of terror was gone. He could meet Stone daily, and Stone would never know who he was. Stone would tire of the fruitlessness of his search and leave. A week, two perhaps. It made no difference. All he had to do was to make sure that Valerie and the boy stayed hidden.

He looked about him with satisfaction. The city was his, and only a short while ago he had tortured himself with the thought of losing everything.

He unlocked the front door, and Chris looked up. He had a searching regard in his eyes that rubbed Tanner the wrong way. Tanner thought irritably, he's getting worse as he gets older. He said, "Where is your mother?"

"In her room," the boy said indifferently.

A frown settled on Tanner's face. The kid was much worse the last couple days. Whatever thread was between them seemed to have been snapped. Vaguely annoyed, he crossed to the bedroom door, and opened it.

Valerie ran across the room and flung her arms about him. He pressed his face against the hollow of her throat, smelling the sweetness of her flesh. She kissed him hard and long, and he felt the softness of her breasts pressed against his chest. Contact such as this usually started his pulses hammering, but there was something wrong in this caress. Her clinging had a desperate quality to it as though she were trying to escape into him. There was a vast change in her the last few days, too, and he thought, it's Stone. He's got her a little crazy.

He pushed her away and held her at arm's length. He wanted to see her face when he told her they were safe. Before he spoke, his eyes caught a splash of color on the bedspread. He turned his head and stared at it. He knew every piece of her clothing, for he selected them himself, but he had never seen this dress or hat before. The dress was of red velvet, rich with color and softness. The hat was made of the same material, ornamented with long ostrich plumes.

His hands slid down to her arms to her wrists, and

his fingers felt the bone. "Where did you get them?" he asked in a strangled voice.

Her face grew frightened at his expression. "Zachary," she cried. "I know you want to select my clothes. But I couldn't pass up this sale."

His fingers dug deeper. "Where?" he repeated.

"Zachary," she moaned. "You're hurting me." The wildness was growing in his eyes, and she had to do something to take his attention from her. "Look at them, Zachary. They're my color. Wait until you hear what I paid for them."

"Valerie," he said in a half scream.

She tried to shrink from him, and he jerked her back. "Down town," she whispered through trembling lips. "There was a sale—"

He raised his left hand and viciously struck her across the face. He struck her again before he let go of her, and she fell across the bed. She pressed a hand against her red and white mottled cheek, and tears streaked her face. He bent over her, and she screamed, "Zachary," trying to crawl from him.

He grabbed her arm and said in a terrible voice, "God-damn you. You went out after I told you not to. You went out knowing Stone is in town."

Her face was pallid, and she stared at him with eyes that were now dry. Her fear of him had wiped away the tears.

"Zachary," she said in a voice that was barely audible. "No one saw me. I wore a heavy veil. There were only women at the sale."

Her words meant nothing to him. He could think of only one thing—she had gone out against his order. Stone could have seen her and remembered her walk or some little mannerism about her.

He raised his hand to strike her again, and a screaming, clawing fury fastened on his left leg.

"You let my mother alone." Chris was half screaming, half sobbing. His small fists beat futilely at Tanner's leg.

Tanner swung his arm, hitting the boy across the face and chest. The blow had the impact of a club, and it tore Chris loose from his leg, knocking him the few feet into a wall. The sound of his head hitting it was sharp and ugly. His scream rose high, then broke into a low moan. He slumped at the base of the wall, his head joining his body at a queer angle. The moaning stopped, and there was no movement in his body.

Tanner said sharply, "Get up." He had hit the boy harder than he intended, but not as hard as the boy pretended.

He started toward him, and Valerie jumped up off the bed and ran past him. She knelt beside Chris and gathered him into her arms. "Chris, Chris." She said the name over and over in a sort of senseless babble.

She stopped and stared into his face. She looked up at Tanner, and her face was stunned. "He's dead," she whimpered. "He's dead."

"He can't be," Tanner said in an incredulous voice. "I didn't hit him that hard."

She straightened, and her eyes were insane. "You

174

killed him," she screamed. She flew at him, her fingernails hooking at his face.

He caught one wrist and missed the other. A set of nails raked his cheek, and in his agitation he did not notice the pain.

"Valerie," he pleaded. "Listen to me."

She jerked free from his grasp and backed from him. Her hair was down around her face, and her eyes were those of a mad woman. "You killed him," she said again. "I'll find Ross. I'll tell him."

He saw the hatred in those mad eyes and knew there was no dealing with it. His senses were sharpened by this new and deadly threat.

She was turning to run, and he yelled, "Valerie." It stopped and swung her about, and his hand plucked the derringer from his vest pocket. If she saw the gun, it did not change the wild hatred on her face.

The sound of the gun was small and brittle, like the snapping of a dry branch. A spasm of pain twisted her face, and it looked as though she were trying to reach him. Her knees buckled with the first step, and she fell in a crumpled heap, one cheek against the floor. Her hair spilled across her face, hiding it from him, and he was relieved he did not have to look at it. He watched her for a long moment and saw no movement.

He stepped through the door and closed it behind him. It was better when he could not see them. He had no time to mourn the woman he had once loved so well, for he had too many things to think of at once.

He had to get rid of their bodies, and no one must

know. His mind worked furiously on the problem. He could say he sent them to San Francisco, to any place, and with this transient population, no one would even be mildly curious. He was a man of standing, no one would question his word, not even Graham. He paced about the room as he thought about how to dispose of them. He could get a stage, drive it to the house after dark, and take them away in it. That might cause a little wonder, but they were his stages. He could do as he pleased with them. Somewhere along that mountain road he could drop them. And in those sheer deep drops, they would never be discovered.

He stopped at the front window and looked down the street. He stared at the figure coming up it, and a creeping coldness froze his muscles and dried the saliva in his mouth. Stone was a dozen steps nearer the house before Tanner moved. He made a sound, and it rattled dryly in his throat. There was a purpose in every deliberate stride made. He knew who lived in this house. It showed in every line of his body.

Tanner whirled from the window and ran toward the back door. Let Stone find them. The shock would first delay him. It would take more time for him to trace their connection to Zachary Tanner. The time should be long enough for him to reach his office and scoop up all available money. He could no longer stay in Virginia City. But a little start and the money would be all he needed.

He was filled with hatred for the dead woman. Her actions had led to all this. He was filled with hatred for

Stone. He felt physically ill from the intensity of his hatred. Damn them both. The words were unspoken, but they pounded in his head like the beat of a great drum. He opened the back door and ran across the yard.

Chapter Eighteen

Ross had not varied that slow, deliberate stride in the last two blocks. Graham had wanted nothing in particular. Just the exchange of a few words, a sort of checking up. It would be a lot different, Ross thought grimly, if Graham knew what was on his mind.

He stopped fifty yards from the house and stared at it. There was a tight fist holding his guts, and he could not rightly say what was uppermost in his mind. What was he going to say or do to her when he saw her? Months ago, the answer to that had been big and black in his mind. He could have killed both her and Anson with little compunction. But he had changed under the slow molding of the days. He shook his head. He would have to decide each step after he saw her and the boy.

He moved toward the house, then stopped. That small, dry sound could have been the report of a gun. He waited and did not hear it again. He was not even certain it came from the house. He broke off the thought, knowing he was standing here deliberately killing time because he dreaded the coming moment of meeting. The conviction came to him with odd shock.

He did dread it. How would Chris react? What if the boy preferred to stay with his mother? He could make the choice against a man who was a stranger to him. I'll take him anyway, Ross thought. I won't be a stranger to him long.

He stared at the house and saw no movement behind the windows. Those windows seemed like blank eyes staring back at him. He shrugged in sudden irritation. Better to get it over with.

He stepped up onto the porch and rapped sharply. The echo faded away and aroused no answering response. He knocked again, having the queer feeling it was useless, that no one would answer the knock. An empty house always had an odd aura about it. This house had partially that feel, and he could not say what the rest of it was.

He tried the door knob and it turned under his hand. He guiltily looked around him before he let the door open further. No one was watching him, the street was empty.

He stepped inside and shut the door behind him. The house was heavy with a brooding silence. He said a tentative, "Hello," and it echoed mockingly and then faded.

He moved deeper into the parlor, noting the luxury of the room. If no one was here, he would wait. He scowled at the thought that Ida might be wrong.

He jerked his head about at the tiny sound coming from the room to his right. It was a low, fluttering sound, tracing its icy fingers along his skin.

He stepped to the door, every nerve stretched tight.

He opened it, looked into the room, and then froze.

The woman lay on the floor, face up, and the long, black hair obscured most of her features. The side of her dress was stained with blood, and little tentacles of it extended along the floor. For a moment, he was certain Ida was wrong, and the thought brought him relief. He knelt beside the woman and gently brushed the hair from her face. The relief was gone. How well he knew those familiar features. He looked at the closed eyes, the ugly pallor of her face and knew she was dead. Then her lips moved, and that small, fluttering sound occurred again.

He knew mixed emotion as he watched her. There had been a few happy months with her, and the memory of them was a powerful force at the moment. He should be remembering how her discontent started before Chris was born, how it had steadily increased until she ran away with Anson, but now the happier memories had the greater force. He felt an agony of hurt and loneliness. The trail was ended, and the futility of everything hit him heavily.

He touched the still hand, and the muscles in his face jerked. He felt warmth in the flesh, and somehow it shocked him. He said unbelievingly, "Valerie," and her eyelids fluttered open.

She stared unseeingly at him before comprehension dawned in her eyes. "Ross," she whispered. "I think I always knew you would catch up with us."

Her hand lay in his, limp and almost lifeless. Her eyes shut, and he was sure she was gone.

She reopened her eyes, and he could see the infinite amount of effort it took. He said in a shaking voice, "Valerie, I'm going after a doctor."

She shook her head, a tiny motion of complete negation. "It would do no good, Ross." A tiny flame burned hotly in her eyes. "Find Anson, Ross. Kill him for what he did to Chris."

His throat was choked, and he was afraid to ask the question. "What did he do to Chris?" The words came out hoarse and strained.

That was pity in her eyes. "Chris is dead. He tried to stop Anson from hurting me, and Anson killed him. Don't let him get away."

Everything went out of him, and he felt tired and beaten. He had made a promise to Lynn, but how could he keep it now? If Anson left town, he would have to follow him.

"He calls himself Zachary Tanner here, Ross."

Tanner! The man who owned the stageline and the biggest saloon in town. Now, Ross understood Mack's connection with all of this, and he remembered where he had seen that dance-hall girl. She had stared at him so intently in Tanner's saloon.

"Tanner shot you?"

Her nod was so small he barely caught it. "I was trying to get to you, to tell you what he had done to Chris. He shot me. He killed Cleve, too. He told me he did."

Her eyes closed, and her face looked white and still. He put an arm under her head and lifted it. He put his cheek close to her lips and was not sure he felt the fan of her breathing.

She said, "Ross . . . about Chris. I tried so hard—" Her eyes were open again, looking steadily at him. The flame, burning in them, was fading, and she spoke in a breathless rush as though she were afraid there was not time to say everything.

"Nothing but work, Ross. That's all you had time for. You were gone so much of the day. And you were always so tired. Tired," she murmured again as though the repeating of the word would make him understand.

He felt a lump form tight and choking in his throat as he saw a little of her side. She had been so young, when they were married, so full of life and gaiety. She had been used to life in a town, and the carving of a new ranch was hard and lonely work. The thought hit him with a clear and revealing flash.

"It's all right, Valerie," he muttered.

His words put a momentary brilliance into her eyes, and her hand tightened feebly upon his. Pain twisted her face, and the brilliance faded. "Ross," she gasped. "In the drawer over there. Money. Most of it is yours."

He spoke the question he had been dreading to ask. "Where is Chris, Valerie?"

She stared at him wonderingly. "Why, here with me." She pushed up a little from his arm, then fell back. Her mouth sagged open, and the eyes went blank and unseeing.

He stood up and stared fixedly at her face. He turned his head and saw the boy, hidden until then by the bed.

He moved to him on slow, stiff legs and stared down at him a long moment before he knelt beside him. He took one of the limp hands in his and said, "Chris," in a harsh, choked voice. He had known him for such a little while. The grief hit him then, real and tearing, and his eyes were hot and stinging. How long he remained in that silent communion, he did not know, but when he rose to his feet, his eyes were dry, and the grief was dull.

He started for the door, then remembered the money she had spoken of. If Tanner left Virginia City, Ross would need it to follow him.

He found the money under a stack of clothing. He counted two thousand dollars from the sheaf of bills. That belonged to him, that was the amount she and Anson had taken before their flight. There was more, but he put it back, wanting only what was his.

He looked back at them from the door. Perhaps he had known all along that he would never really catch up with them. He shut the door softly behind him as though he dreaded to disturb something. He would return for them later, but first, there was Tanner to find.

He went down the street, his face so set that it looked all harsh angles. Passersby looked at that hard and bitter face and moved away from him. He did not even see them. At the moment, he did not think, he did not feel; he only moved.

Lynn saw him as he neared Graham's office. She hurriedly crossed the street and caught his ann. He looked at her with no recognition in his eyes.

"Ross," she said. "I've been watching Graham's office for you, trying to learn if the woman had been found. I don't think she has. Graham hasn't left his office all afternoon." She saw no indication that he even heard her, and she asked sharply, "Ross, what is it?"

He looked at her with bemused eyes, then said slowly, "Lynn, I found them." He thought she did not quite understand and added, "Chris and the woman who was my wife."

Her face went blank and still. "Ah," she said in a voice that held nothing.

"They're dead, Lynn. Anson killed them both."

He saw the hurt for him in her eyes as she asked, "Is he still here?"

"I think he is," he said slowly. Tanner should be unless he had left in immediate flight. Ross doubted that. Tanner would not leave what he had built without trying to salvage something from it.

He started to move away, and she would not release his arm. "Wait, Ross," she breathed.

His face was hard as he looked at her. She could not talk him out of this.

She said, "Tell Graham. Ross, listen. After this is over, don't you want to stay here? You won't be able to, unless Graham knows."

He turned the words over in his mind, reluctant to be side-tracked for even a moment. He stared at her, seeing what she was offering. After this was over he did want to stay in Virginia City. He wanted to help Redford with his claim, he wanted to be near her. If

Graham did not know the circumstances before Tanner died, Ross would become a hunted man.

He said, "Graham can be with or against me, but I'm still going to kill Anson."

She nodded mutely and moved with him toward the door of Graham's office.

Graham frowned as he saw them. It deepened at the expressions on their faces, and his hands gripped the edge of his desk. "What is it now?" he growled.

Ross told him in a dispassionate voice of the long hunt and its cause. "The man I'm looking for is here," he said. "He killed a woman last night and my wife and son a short while ago to hide his identity."

Graham looked from one face to the other. Lynn nodded and said, "It's true." Some of Graham's hostility faded under the flat ring of truth in the words. His manner was uncertain as he asked, "Who is he?"

"He calls himself Zachary Tanner here," Ross answered.

"No," Graham yelped. "My God, if you think you can come here and pick anyone you want—"

Ross locked eyes with him. "I'm going to kill him. You can come with me, if you want. He may talk before he dies. Don't try to stop me." The last was as metallic sounding as hammer against iron.

Lynn moved to Graham and said, "Go with him."

Graham searched her face, and something in what Ross said or in her manner reached him. He picked up his hat and said grimly, "I'll go. I'm holding you accountable for everything that happens."

Lynn started to go with them, and Ross shook his head. "Wait here," he said. He looked at the strain in her face. He wanted to talk to her, to tell her of the promise in the future. But there was no time.

He said gently, "It will be all right, Lynn." The rest of the things could be said later.

He went down the street with Graham, and neither of them spoke. Graham's breathing was heavy, and Ross could feel the hostility flowing from the man.

They walked into the saloon, and it was filling up for the evening's business. A floorman saw them, and something in their faces drew him toward them.

Graham growled at him, "Stay here. Don't let anyone up those stairs."

Ross looked back at the door, leading to the stairs. Every face in the room was turned toward him, and all motion was arrested. Graham being with him helped that much. He would not have to fight the entire place.

He went up the stairs with a deliberate motion, Graham at his heels. The sound of Graham's breathing was louder in the narrow hall.

He moved to the door at the end of the hall. He stopped and listened and thought he could hear the sound of feverish activity behind it. That squeak, then a louder, sharper sound could only be made by a drawer being opened and closed.

He said in a low voice, "Stay here." He drew his gun and put his left hand on the knob. The end of the long trail was here. His anger and hating were fused into a rock-hard determination to get this over.

He turned the knob and opened the door. He was two steps into the room, and the figure behind the desk had not looked up.

"Anson," he said.

The man looked at the crouched figure. His hands were filled with papers and money, and they held motionless above the opened bag on the desk. Papers littered the desk top and floor, and most of the drawers stood open. His face went bloodless. His lips moved, but no sound came from them.

"Anson," Ross said again.

The man's eyes darted frantically from the gun in Ross's hand to the one lying on the desk-top, near the bag. There was another in the half opened top drawer, and both were so terribly far out of reach. He opened his hands and let their contents flutter to the desk and floor. He swallowed hard and said in a squeaky voice, "You've got the wrong man."

"Have I, Anson?" Ross asked. "The woman who worked for you didn't think so. Cleve didn't think so. Valerie didn't, either. She wasn't dead, Anson."

Anson's breath came out in a long-drawn sigh. His eyes were riveted to the gun on the desk. Did the high back of the desk hide it from Stone? He was afraid to grab for it.

He raised his eyes to Ross's face, and his lips moved in a heavy sigh. "I guess I knew you would catch up with me someday." His hands were steadier, and his voice had more strength. He was face to face with the inevitable.

His eyes lighted, and he cried, "I can make you rich. Richer than you ever dreamed of. I'll give you half—" The words trailed away as he saw no reaction on that hard face. "No?" he said, and a faint, wry smile twisted his lips.

His eyes darted to the gun. If only he dared grab for it. He correctly read the purpose in that hard face, and his own was wet with sweat. He could feel the moisture trickling down inside the neckband of his shirt. As long as Stone would listen, he could still buy time with his words. He said pleadingly, "Stone, I loved her."

He saw the twist of Stone's face and went on frantically, "I did. From the moment I saw her. It was something no one could change. I loved the boy, too. I didn't mean to kill him."

Ross's face turned raw and violent, and Tanner threw out a hand. "Wait," he pleaded. "We could have been happy, if you'd left us alone. Even while we were running, there were moments—" His voice trailed away.

The hating was alive on Ross's face. In a way, what Anson said was true. But did a man step in and smash another's life and expect no repayment? He could pull the trigger and end this, but the hating would not let him. A bullet was too quick.

He said, "Step away from the desk, Anson." He wanted to break this man with his hands; he wanted to make it as slow and hurting as possible.

Anson stared at him, and Ross snapped, "Move." He motioned with the gun, and Anson obeyed its command. He backed along the wall, his eyes never leaving Stone.

"You wouldn't shoot me down without a chance?" he begged.

"I should," Ross growled and slipped the gun in its holster.

Anson's eyes lighted with renewed hope. He came off the wall in a rush, and his desperateness lent him strength. The savagery of his attack beat Ross back several steps, and he took two hard blows before he could set himself. A cornered man was a man two-fold strong, and Anson proved it by the way he absorbed Ross's blows. Ross slugged him in the face, knowing raw, vicious satisfaction each time his knuckles landed. Blood seeped through Anson's beard and colored his face. The flow thickened, changing the color of his beard, then dripped onto his shirt-front. He took the blows with no outcry, not even a grunt, and always he bored in. The vigor of his attack was an awesome thing, and Ross used all his strength in breaking and throwing it back.

Both men's breathing was hoarse and clogged, and red bubbles broke at Anson's mouth with each breath. But his vitality was ebbing, he did not bounce back from each blow as readily as he had.

Ross took a deep breath and plodded forward, brutally slogging Anson with each step. Anson's strength seemed to go all at once. He took a brutal blow in the belly and folded over. He took a staggering step in the general direction of the desk, and his buckling knees could not support the weight of his upper body. He spilled to the floor, and when he tried to rise, he could get no higher than his hands and knees.

"Get up," Ross snarled. He wanted to kill this man, wanted to kill him with his bare hands.

"I can't," Anson whimpered. But he was trying. He crawled a few feet to a chair and using it as a support, rose to his knees. Ross watched him with hard eyes. He felt no pity for him.

Anson's hands seized the back of the chair. His back straightened, and he lifted and flung the chair. It flew through the air a foot off the floor, and Ross could not avoid it. He jumped, but the chair legs became entangled with his feet. He went down hard, the swearing rattling in his throat at the way Anson had taken him in.

He kicked the chair aside and heard the rush of Anson's boots. He was sure Anson would dive upon him, and he braced himself against the crushing weight. But Anson was running toward the desk. He grabbed up the gun, lying on the desk-top and whirled toward Ross. Triumph was blazing in his eyes as he raised the gun.

Ross rolled to free his right arm. He had misjudged his man, and it could cost him dear. He clawed for the gun in its holster, and his awkward position hampered his movement.

Anson fired too quickly. The bullet thwocked into the plank flooring beside Ross's face, filling his cheek with stinging splinters.

His gun was out and leveled before Anson fired the second shot. He pulled the trigger, and the bullet took Anson in the chest, slamming him backward into the desk. His arm flung up, and he fired again, but it was a shot fired by reflex action and not aim. It sang wide of Ross's head, burying itself in the wall. The desk screeched along the floor as Anson's weight moved it. His body bent, and it looked as though he were falling. He straightened with terrible effort, but he could not raise the gun. It sagged lower and lower in the drooping arm, and the strain of will against fading muscle power etched deep lines in his face.

Ross did not fire again. He watched Anson's struggle with curious, detached eyes.

Anson's hand opened, and he dropped the gun. He stared at Ross with glazing eyes, then coughed. He swayed back and forth and said, "To think I was ever afraid of you."

He took a step toward the corner of the desk, his weight coming down hard on his heel. "It wasn't necessary—" The words broke off, and he bent at the waist. He fell slowly, the upper half of his body coming down on top of the desk. It hung there for a moment, then rolled off and crashed to the floor.

Ross slowly shook his head. He stared at his gun, then put it away. He did not know Graham was beside him until he spoke.

"I heard him," Graham said in an unbelieving voice. He stared at the figure on the floor. "Most of us never knew this side at all. There was a lot of good in him."

He shook his head. "A man never knows anything for sure." He looked at Ross and said gruffly, "You ready?"

Ross nodded and turned toward the door. He was aware of the outbreak of voices below him. He had not heard them until then.

"Quiet down there," Graham yelled and moved out in front of him.

Weariness laid hold of Ross as he walked behind him. He was glad that Graham was here, glad that Graham would take care of the questions, the confusion. At some time in the future he would examine all this, but now his mind was a void. He had one more bad moment ahead of him, when he returned to that house after Chris and Valerie. But Lynn was here to help him, and his face brightened as he thought of her. He picked up his step. She was waiting now. It was over for all of them, and only the bright promise of what lay ahead remained.

Center Point Publishing
600 Brooks Road ● PO Box 1
Thorndike ME 04986-0001 USA

(207) 568-3717

US & Canada:
1 800 929-9108
www.centerpointlargeprint.com